Seven By Seven

Seven Deadly Tales
Of the Seven Deadly Sins
From Seven Deadly Authors

Edited by Tony Burton

SEVEN BY SEVEN

ISBN 0-9778-4020-4

First printing – April 2006
Wolfmont Publishing,
Copyright ©2006 Wolfmont Publishing
All Rights Reserved

For information, contact:
info@wolfmont.com
or
Wolfmont Publishing
PO Box 205
Ranger, GA   30734

Cover illustration adapted from
The Table of the Seven Deadly Sins
by Heironymus Bosch, circa 1490

The illustrations preceding each section are
taken from *Le grant kalendrier des Bergiers*
printed by Nicolas le Rouge, Troyes, 1496

Foreword

Writing a short story is never easy. Writing shorter than the usual and retaining all the elements of theme, plot, setting, and character is downright hard. In this impressive full-length volume, seven experienced mystery writers each take on that difficult task seven times over. They additionally struggle to fulfill an essential parameter set for them by the editor: to produce stories on themes chosen *for* them rather than *by* them.

All of the seven authors here have managed to succeed in their attempts, and for the readers—us—they show something of the internal dynamic a writer must engage in, in order to produce a story that satisfies both the creator and his/her audience. These stories, because they can be compared and contrasted within a same-theme series, as well as within each set produced by a single author, demonstrate a great deal about the writing process.

Constructing mysteries or crime stories is a bit different than creating other kinds of stories, because above and beyond any additional theme set for a story or a collection, a single consideration underlies the entire genre: a question of justice. The mystery or crime story always brings to bear a point of view on human misdeeds and their consequences. Sometimes the author seeks to represent society in delivering some retribution, and sometimes the one crafting the piece chooses a more morally neutral tone, as nature itself seems to in assessing the interplay between predator and prey.

What interested me in reading this particular collection was how the authors chose to handle this particular genre issue. Each of them grappled with how judgments would be made and justice delivered. And that, for me, is the essential rationale for reading and writing mystery or crime fiction, to come to a new comprehension of or to paint a viewpoint on this issue. Here, with the "sins" so archetypal and so particularly chosen in each story, the writers have been able to wrestle with the ethics involved in very focused and particular ways.

Overwhelmingly, I think that what these seven authors display is not a condemnation of their characters and their sins. They go beyond the pre-Christian and then Medieval concepts of blaming, or casting stones, to a higher-minded stance of understanding and compassion for their flawed human characters. That, in fact, is the writer's job, to get into the mind of the villain as well as the hero, to display these individuals' inner workings, and to allow us to see why certain actions result from complex external situations triggering personal and species-wide internal states.

Our seven craftsmen here thus render justice and judgment in the highest sense. They allow their sinning characters simply to reap the results of their own actions. And though the Medieval mind, as Tony Burton shows us, sees the punishment for sinning man as harsh, the crime writing artists represented in this book take a stance that justice is a simple affair. Those who indulge in the lower emotions and actions arising from our very human, but shadowy side will inexorably and simply reap the results of what they sow.

These glimpses into the creative process and examinations of the fruits of human negativity are well worth the reading. In essence then, these are morality tales. Be entertained, but be guided.

G. Miki Hayden, 2004 Edgar winner for "The Maids" in *Blood on Their Hands*

Introduction

Welcome to **Seven By Seven**, a compendium of flash fiction pieces, all focused on the seven deadly sins, and written by seven different authors. Each author's unique viewpoint on the various deadly sins makes for very intriguing reading. I believe you will enjoy these stories as much as I have.

Some people are not familiar with the concept and history of the seven deadly sins, so here is a short primer on their beginnings and how they have developed over the centuries.

Originally, there were eight *Thoughts of Evil*, or as described by St. John Cassian, *Eight Principal Vices*. These were Gluttony, Fornication, Avarice, Wrath, Sadness, Sloth, Vainglory, and Pride. That listing, by the way, places them in ascending order of importance, Pride being the worst of the eight. He codified these eight vices around 420 CE.

In the late Sixth Century, Pope Gregory I made the change from the Eight Principal Vices to the Seven Deadly Sins in his writing, *Moralia in Job*. He lists them as Lust, Gluttony, Sadness, Avarice, Anger, Envy and Pride. Note that they changed. In fact, later in the Middle Ages the sin of Sadness was replaced with the sin of Sloth. It may be because, in that time and place, with the Goths, Visigoths, Huns, marauding Norsemen and the Black Death, being sad was an inevitable part of the human condition.

It should be noted that there are also Seven Cardinal Virtues, which are in direct opposition to the Seven Deadly Sins. These are Chastity, Moderation, Charity, Zeal, Meekness, Generosity, and Humility.

In the medieval mind, each sin was associated with a very specific punishment in the afterlife. For example, those guilty of the sin of Lust were smothered in burning brimstone and fire by demons. Those guilty of the sin of Envy were submersed in frigid water and held there by chortling, perhaps parka-clad, demons.

One can only imagine the confusion that must have arisen in the demonic hordes when a new denizen arrived in Hell, who had spent his or her life in equal devotion to both Envy and Lust.

Were they shuffled from arctic waters to burning pits of brimstone, flip-flopping back and forth? Or perhaps the demons quarreled over what to do with them, while the condemned sinners languished in some sort of infernal waiting room, listening to eternal, hellish Muzak.

That might have been as horrible a punishment as being dismembered alive, which was the specified reward for Wrath. You will find illustrations at the beginning of each section, that show some medieval artists' conceptions of how each sin was punished in Hell.

Throughout the years, the Seven Deadly Sins have been the roots of various artistic endeavors. The cover of this book is adapted from a painting by Hieronymus Bosch, *The Table of the Seven Deadly Sins*. There have been plays, movies, songs, music groups and even a video game based upon the concepts of these very specific offenses against the Almighty.

In spite of that, I believed that the authors who contributed to this anthology were creative enough and inventive enough to come up with new thoughts, new representations and new stories of those sins and how they make themselves manifest in humanity. I am now sure I was right, and I am proud to be associated with this group of Seven Deadly Authors.

So, go ahead – turn the page, and enjoy your trip through 49 short tales of the transgressions that top the charts of Hell – **Seven By Seven**.

Oh, and a final warning: ***Don't be tempted!***

The Editor,

Charles A. "Tony" Burton

A medieval German illustration of
demons representing the
Seven Deadly Sins, circa 1511

Lust

The lustful being smothered in fire and
brimstone in Hell.

Signature Lick

by Sunny Frazier

I thought Jesse's fascination with the guitar would be a flirtation. When he bought the Fender Stratocaster, I knew it was love.

At first, his virgin fumbling with the strings was hard on the ear. I watched his fingers struggle with the chords, stretching to reach the frets. Over time, after he learned a few songs, it became romantic. I was his audience. When he put the instrument down and came to bed, I relished the calluses on his fingertips against my soft skin.

Jesse got a gig with a cover band. It satisfied him for awhile, but it was never enough. He spent $2000 of our savings on a Marshall "full stack." The speakers, topped with an amp, were like a big, black refrigerator in my living room. It was a monolith of sound. I realized his music had evolved from a hobby to an obsession.

He graduated from basic rock and set his sights higher. It wasn't enough to be adept playing other people's music. He searched for a unique style, a sound that flowed from his soul. "Three chords and the truth," Keith Richards dubbed it. Carlos Santana had it. Eric Clapton had it. A sound so distinctive any listener could identify the artist by the first notes. Jesse sought out his signature lick.

I watched Jesse's struggle as he literally tried to amplify his thoughts into his music. He developed a core of fans in the small towns of central California. I went to every club, stood at the perimeter of the crowd, praised him after each performance. I was proud to be his "old lady." Clayton had his Layla, McCartney had Michelle, Buddy Holly had Peggy Sue. I was Jesse's muse. Someday, he would immortalize me in song.

The break we'd been waiting for came at the end of the third year. A Los Angeles club wanted Jesse, but as a solo act. There would be a booking agent in the audience, a possible record deal.

"I don't want you to come," Jesse told me. "I need to be on my game. You're a distraction." He said it in the sexy voice he used when bantering with the crowd between numbers. It was seductive, and he knew it.

As he was packing his equipment, he pulled out a handgun. I knew he owned a weapon, but I'd never seen it.

"I want you to carry this for protection while I'm away." Our separation suddenly seemed threatening, the neighborhood less friendly. I'd never been alone since I'd moved in with Jesse at 19. I tucked the gun into my canvas tote.

By the end of three days, I was beyond missing Jesse. I couldn't sleep. The empty house made strange noises. Eyes seemed to follow me as I walked through the neighborhood.

When I couldn't stand it any longer, I jumped in the car and headed for Los Angeles. I arrived just at the last set finished.

"He went back to the hotel," said a member of the house band. He smirked.

The front desk wouldn't give me Jesse's room number. They phoned his room, but he didn't answer.

There were four floors. I went down the corridor of each one, calling his name.

I passed a room on the third floor. At first, I didn't hear it over the noise of the ice machine. I retraced my steps to room 3042. From behind the door came a giggle, answered by the sound of seduction. The signature lick.

I pulled the gun out of my tote before I knocked.

here He Shouldn't Be

by Frank Zafiro

Light flickered on the screen. Tate stared up at it,
watching with detachment as the woman there faked
pleasure. Badly.

Men stood and changed seats. Over and over.
Different men. Always moving, searching.

He watched the screen, but saw everything out of his
peripheral vision.

I shouldn't be here.

He thought of Kathy, at home with the kids.
Probably on the phone with her sister. Or doing a
crossword. She thought he was working late.

A man sat down in the seat behind him, just off to the
right. He could smell the man's musky cologne.

The woman on the screen changed positions with
workmanlike precision. Her breasts bounced with
each motion, but Tate stared instead at the male
actor's buttocks as they flexed and thrust.

I shouldn't be here. I should be home, working in my den. Helping Emily with her homework. Any place but here.

Hardly anyone came to these places anymore. It was all available on cable TV or DVDs or the Internet. But cable didn't have what he wanted. And Kathy would find his DVDs. She would see where he went on the Internet.

That's what this place was, he realized. A last bastion of anonymity. Fulfilling. Dangerous.

I shouldn't be here. I shouldn't want this.

He struggled with it constantly. Every day, he tried to overwhelm it with work. Tons of work. He cultivated his public image. A wife. Family. Friends. Even a mistress. When all of that failed, he pushed it away with alcohol.

But his feelings, his desires, were relentless.

The man behind moved up to his row and sat two seats away.

His breath quickened.

On screen, the naked man pounded. The woman faked.

The man slipped into the chair beside him. In the cool theater, Tate could sense the warmth of his closeness.

Moments passed.

The man leaned towards him. Touched his knee with his own.

When Tate didn't object, things progressed. A touch, a caress, the rustle of cloth.

He trembled and stared at the screen. Mouth dry, he held his breath.

He knew he should get up. Get up and leave. It wasn't right to want this. It wasn't right to feel this way.

I shouldn't be—

Touching. Then a blur of motion.

He let out a guttural moan, unable to contain his reaction. It was so...so...

Oh...my...GOD!

His eyelids fluttered closed.

Kathy did it sometimes, rarely, but not like this. Not so right.

So wrong!

He didn't care. His head lolled backward. He stared up into the darkness. He was tired of fighting it. Tired of the passion that drove him and the guilt that came behind.

Another low, shuddering moan escaped his lips. He felt a rush of tension throughout his whole body, building up, building up—

Intense white light blasted into his face. He recoiled, squinting.

"All right, pervs." The intonation of resigned authority filled the voice. "Knock it off."

The other man snapped upright. Both of them sat stock-still, staring straight ahead.

"Just watching the movie, officer," the other man said.

The light left Tate's face and shone toward his lap.

"That what you're calling it now?"

"We—"

"Shut up."

The light drifted back to his face and hovered there. He glanced sidelong into the light, shivering from fear and excitement.

"Oh, shit," the police officer muttered.

His heart sank. *I shouldn't be here.*

"Councilman Tate? Is that really you?"

rue Colors

by John M. Floyd

"He's dead," Nicole Finney said. Teary-eyed, she led
Officers Payne and Tyler down a dim hallway.
Morris Dunn lay facedown in his office.

"This happened when?" Payne asked.

"Ten minutes ago."

"What'd you see?"

Nicole drew a shaky breath. "Nothing. I was up
front at my desk, with the copier repairman, when we
heard shots. We thought Mr. Dunn was the only
other person in the building."

"Go on."

"Well, when I got back here, whoever did it was
gone. But the copier guy... he said he saw the killer.
Holding a gun."

"He saw him?"

"Her. He talks funny, but this was clear. He said, 'It
was a woman. A woman with wet hair.'"

The officers exchanged glances. It had been raining all day. Whoever killed Dunn must've just come inside.

The frightened repairman had left, Nicole said. Tyler quickly phoned in orders to locate him. Meanwhile, employees Hilda Harper and Pam Brady stomped in with rain hats and umbrellas. Their hair–Harper's gray, Brady's blond–was as dry as Nicole's. They received the news in stunned silence.

When asked, Nicole revealed that there was also a back entrance, from a covered garage. "I can only see the front door from my desk," she said, "but anyone entering the back has to key in a door code."

Then, a break: Dunn's appointment book. He was to meet his wife at noon today–around the time of the murder.

"Describe the wife," Officer Payne said.

Nicole wiped her eyes. "Nice enough lady. Fiftyish, redheaded, hot-tempered."

"Seen her today?"

"No. If she was here, she used the back door. She and the employees all know the code."

Suddenly a woman swept in, using that very door.

"I'm late, Nicole, is Morris–"

Mrs. Dunn stopped short. The policemen solemnly informed her of her husband's death, then stepped away. "Her hair's dry too," Tyler whispered. "And check this out."

Another appointment-book entry said: HILDA'S EXIT INTERVIEW 4 P.M.

"Looks like Hilda Harper's getting the axe."

Over the next hour they questioned everyone. Mrs. Dunn had been shopping all morning, the stony-faced Ms. Harper was resentful about being fired (enough to shoot her boss?), and the attractive young Pam Brady appeared more upset by Dunn's death than his wife was. This suspicion was verified by Nicole Finney.

"Yes," she said, "Pam and Mr. Dunn were having an affair. And yes, Mrs. Dunn knew. So did Pam's husband."

Not that that helped the case. Betrayed spouses are often vengeful, but Mrs. Dunn's hair didn't look rained-on, and even if Pam Brady's husband came here today soaking wet, the person the repairman saw in the hallway had been female. There was no solid evidence against anyone. Mrs. Dunn and the employees were allowed to leave.

"So how'd the killer get in?" Tyler said, as the lab team wrapped up. "The wet-hair description suggests the front door, but it was in plain view. And the back door requires a code."

The officers were pondering that when the copier repairman was brought in.

"I told Mith Finney what I thaw," he said. "The woman had wet hair. And a pithtol."

"Your name, sir?"

"John Wandolph."

Payne looked up from his notepad. "John Randolph?"

"That'th wight. Wandolph."

Payne blinked and turned to his partner. "It's Mrs. Dunn. She did it."

"What?"

"He talks funny, Nicole said. Remember?" Payne jumped to his feet. "The killer didn't have 'wet' hair—she had *red* hair."

Both cops rushed out into the rain. Randolph, left alone and confused in the office, stared after them.

"Who talkth funny?" he said.

A Breech of Trust

by Gary Hoffman

Deputy sheriff Mark Cattleman slipped quietly
through the thick underbrush toward the car. Old
man Riddle had called the sheriff to report a car
pulling into his property. Riddle was eighty-five
years old now and in his younger days would have
handled the situation himself. Riddle was a neighbor
of Mark's, and since Mark was due to get off his shift
soon, the sheriff sent him to investigate.

Mark slipped up to the rear of the car. A grin came
across his face when he saw a pair of feet sticking up
in the air and a bare butt bobbing up and down. It
was a warm spring afternoon and all of the windows
in the car were down. The closer he got, the more he
could hear the grunts and groans of the two people
inside the car. He went to the side of the car where
he would be at the people's heads and looked down
into the face of his wife!

They still didn't realize he was there. He unholstered
his Ruger .357 magnum, put it up against the side of
his wife's head, and cocked it. The man in the car
looked up. "You better get the hell out of here,
mister," Mark drawled out. Even in this situation,
Mark had to smile at the sight of the man running

buck-naked through the thorns and other underbrush.
He looked back at his wife. "Get your clothes on.
We're going home." He made Becky drive the patrol
car home while he held the gun on her.

Nothing was said between the two until they were
home. Mark waved the gun in her direction. "Pick
up the phone and call Walt. Tell him to get up here
right away." Becky Cattleman did as she was told.

Walt lived on a farm just a mile from his parents.
When he got to his parents' house, he found his
mother sitting on the couch and his father sitting
right in front of her on a dining room chair he'd
turned around so he could lean on the back. Mark
still had the gun pointed toward her. "Now you tell
Walter exactly what you have done. You lie, or even
stutter, and what little brains you have will be
splattered all over that wall behind you."

"What the hell's going on?" Walt spouted out.

"Tell him!" Mark shouted at Becky.

Becky jumped at his loud voice, but looked at her
son. "Baby, I made a mistake." She paused. Mark's
hand twitched. "I had sex with a man, and your
daddy caught us." She rattled the words out.

"Oh, my God, Mom."

Mark watched the reaction on his son's face and then
turned back toward Becky. He slowly let the
hammer down. "Now, you've got thirty seconds to
get in your car and get off this property and never
come back. I'll walk out on the front porch in thirty

seconds. If I think you're still within gun range, I'll shoot your sorry ass." He looked at his watch. Becky grabbed her purse, jumped up, and ran.

Years later, when Mark could talk about this incident, he said he made two mistakes that day. His first was not hightailing it into town to beat her to the bank. Becky cleaned out their bank accounts and safe deposit box on her way out of town. The second was, he should have shot her right then and there. Under the mitigating circumstances, he would have served his time and been out of jail by now.

ast Words

by Deborah Elliott-Upton

Rafe remembered the brunette's predictable last words. None of them had understood. It wasn't so much "Why *me*?" as much as "Why *not* you?"

Chained to the basement bench, a blonde had replaced the brunette and waited for his return. He smirked, imagining her certain, but unsuccessful escape attempts. Even nude, she was nothing special – except she now belonged to him.

At work, Rafe revealed no clue to his secret life. His co-workers griped about the mundane routine, but Rafe enjoyed the never-changing job. Growing up, Mother's irrational whims constantly amended The Rules, making him feel stupid and inept when he forgot a new regimen. Flamboyant and decadent, she represented every woman he'd brought to the basement. They had paid for their immorality. Someday, Mother would, too.

The radio's music abruptly ended. As the newscast began, the workroom hushed.

"Chief Atkinson reported that a victim's profile has been difficult to ascertain since the Card Shark Killer has murdered four victims with no common relationships, other than their gender," the announcer said. "The killer, leaving a playing card in the mouth of each victim, has police baffled as to the type of woman he targets."

No common relationships? Idiots, he thought. *Of course, there's a common relationship. They're all lying whores.* He dumped the mail into the cart and shoved it toward the aisle for delivery to the execs upstairs.

The police couldn't even decipher his signature clue. The Card Shark Killer? He hadn't left a nondescript card between their blue lips, but the ace of spades. *The Death Card*, for Pete's sake. He'd probably have to carve a message into the blonde's torso and sign it Death Card Killer for them to get it right.

Why hadn't the police recognized them all as hookers?

He'd taken a chance picking up the last one, especially since her friends may have caught a glimpse of him through the car window. It seemed risky to return there twice in a row, but the temptation grew too strong to resist and besides, they looked stoned.

The blonde resembled Mother when she'd gone platinum. "Variety is the spice of life," she'd said, parading through the living room wearing nothing more than a smile.

Dangerous going back for this one, but worth it. When she leaned into his open window, her nauseating perfume filled the car. Rafe recognized Mother's scent immediately.

"Wanta date?" the blonde asked.

"I want total control," he said.

"Sure," she'd purred. "But, that's extra."

He flashed the money clip and her eyes widened. The hundred sat atop three inches of ones. Just like Mother, he thought. *The greedy never see the truth.*

Reality yanked Rafe from his daydreams. The room had become eerily quiet and emptied of his co-workers.

Suddenly, Rafe was surrounded by black SWAT uniforms. His mouth formed a slight grin. Decked in protective garb, the police feared him, too. As if an unarmed man could overpower them strictly by his will, their arms grasped high-powered weapons aimed at his chest. Rafe laughed.

The familiar surge in his groin strengthened. This was it. No more begging for attention. The media would splash his image and words on TV, in the newspapers and the tabloids. Finally, the lust for total control arrived full-fledged. Finally, he'd have power. Finally, Mother would see *him*. He hoped she'd be afraid.

As he filed past, his boss asked, "Why, Rafe? Why *you?*"

Rafe's smile faltered. "Why *not* me?"

nsubordination

by BJ Bourg

"Here are the numbers, Senator." Rachael Starkey placed the printout on my desk. "You're number one in the polls."

I smiled. Not at the printout, but at Rachael's pink silk shirt. Her collar was open, exposing the tops of her swollen, snowy breasts. A light sprinkle of freckles added character to an already mesmerizing picture. I felt a stirring deep inside my stomach. I smiled again– Ben always hired the best-looking secretaries for me.

"Do you want to go ahead with the debate tomorrow night?"

I tore my gaze from Rachael's cleavage and stared up into her emerald eyes. "Yes, it will continue as scheduled."

Rachael nodded. Her blonde curls dangled near her ears. She turned and rose on her tiptoes to make a notation on the wall calendar. Her smooth, tanned calves contracted and her back arched slightly, pushing her pear-shaped buttocks against her thin skirt. My heart raced. My palms began to sweat.

Rachael dropped to her heels and turned to look down at me. Her brows puckered. "What is it?"

I tore my gaze from her face and slowly scanned down to her ankles and then back up to her eyes.

"Senator, what is going on?"

I stood and stepped toward Rachael. She tried to move back, but the wall stopped her. I reached out with my right hand and gently brushed her shoulder. Rachael's face paled. She stared down at the floor and dipped her shoulder from under my hand. She tried to step around me, but I reached out and pressed my hand against her stomach. It was firm and defined.

"Where are you going?" I asked in a soft voice.

Rachael swallowed hard. "Senator, you're scaring me."

"It's okay."

"Please, just let me—"

I leaned forward quickly and pressed my lips against Rachael's. I pushed my tongue against her pursed lips. She tried to pull away. I wrapped the fingers of my right hand around the back of her head and pulled her to me. She tried to push me away, but I batted her arms down with my left hand. I squeezed her breasts.

"You feel so good," I murmured, my breath hot on Rachael's face. "Come on Sweetie, kiss me."

I pinned Rachael's face back and pushed my lips roughly against hers. I tried to force my tongue into her mouth. A twinge of excitement reverberated down my spine when I felt her lips part. My tongue darted into her mouth. I moaned my pleasure as I felt her cool wetness. Her body relaxed in my arms. I slid my hands upwards and felt the silk shirt rolling beneath my palms. My fingers brushed the bottoms of her breasts and I sighed.

Suddenly, a piercing pain shot through my tongue. Warm blood gushed into my mouth. I shoved Rachael hard against the wall and I heard her gasp. I reached up and shoved my thumbs into her eyes. When she opened her mouth to scream, I pulled my throbbing tongue away and snatched a ceramic vase from my desk. I smashed the vase on Rachael's head and she collapsed in a heap.

My office door burst open and Ben rushed in. He took one look at Rachael and shook his head. "Not again."

I put my sleeve to my bloody mouth. "You know what to do with her."

"Senator, you can't keep doing this. People will start getting suspicious."

"You're right. Maybe you should hire me a male secretary next time."

Ben nodded. "Yes, ma'am. Get yourself cleaned up. I'll take care of this."

ne Night's Dream

by Kimberly Brown

Kate set mugs of ale on the rough wooden table and put her hands on her hips. The noise in the public house was especially raucous this evening. She usually loved it, but this night it bothered her.

Angus reached up to play with the stays of her dress and she pushed him away. The table of men laughed and Tom drew Kate toward him. "It's not your turn tonight," he said to Angus. "Is it, sweet lass?"

Kate slapped at Tom. She loved being admired by the men, watching them as they watched her. At twenty years old, some called her an old maid, but she still felt young and desired. Tonight, though, was different. Tonight she'd heard a rumor that Billy was coming home.

After she brought a round of ale to another group of men--rough sailors from the look of them--Kate heard the front door creak open. Billy!

He looked different after six months away. His skin was leathery from the sun, and his merry blue eyes had lines of worry around them. She watched him as he strode toward her. The table she was serving grew quiet. When, without a word, he took her arm and led her up the stairs, they broke into uproarious laughter.

Billy pushed her into the nearest sleeping chamber and kissed her hard. She kissed him back, as if her lips hadn't felt another's since he had been gone. She hoped he believed that, even if she knew it wasn't so.

He pushed her toward the bed, then stopped her before she lay down. "Look, Kate." From his cloak he pulled a bag and threw it on the bed. His eyes shone in the candlelight. "Look inside."

Kate's trembling fingers unlaced the string and spilled out the contents. Gold coins! "Where..."

Billy held up a hand. "Please, do not ask." He pushed her down on the bed, spilling the gold onto the floor.

* * *

Later, Billy lay in Kate's arms, close to sleep. "Kate," he whispered. "Tomorrow we must go away. Men may be looking for me."

"Men you took the gold from?"

"We'll go south. We'll buy a farm. Have children."

"The gold—" Kate began, but Billy was asleep. Children! As Kate held Billy she wondered if she could have children. She'd visited the village witch many times since she was fourteen, many times took the draught that got rid of a baby. Could she bear Billy's child?

Kate and Billy were both wakened suddenly when the door burst open. Kate sat up and clutched the bedclothes to her. Two men, dirty and greasy, strode forward, pistols pointed at Billy. One of the pistols exploded and Billy fell back, motionless. Kate screamed as blood pumped from his chest.

One man began picking up the gold coins from the floor where they'd fallen. The other approached Kate with a leer.

"Leave her," the man squatting on the floor said sharply. "This'll buy us the company of a fresher woman."

The two left the room and Kate could hear shouts and laughter from the men below. They hadn't heard the shot, or her scream. Or they hadn't cared. She stared at Billy's lifeless face. Nausea twisted her stomach. She couldn't go back down the stairs and laugh with men who hadn't cared what happened to her.

Kate stood and shook out the bedclothes around Billy's body. Perhaps not all the gold had fallen to the floor. Her efforts unearthed three gold coins. Not enough to buy a farm, but enough to take her far away from this place.

The Four Horsemen of the Apocalypse

Gluttony

Gluttons being force-fed rats, snakes and toads in Hell.

Strength of a Dancer

by Frank Zafiro

Sarah moved like a woman a hundred pounds lighter, but then, she once was a dancer.

A beautiful dancer.

Fifteen years old. Her body nubile, lithe but blessed with a young woman's curves. Flat belly, arms and legs corded with hard dancer's muscles.

They say that when you develop muscles at that age, the strength stays with you all of your life. She believed that now.

Sarah slipped on her shirt, crossed the living room, opened the door and hurried down the stairs. No one passed her. She left the apartment building and headed south. Her breath came in ragged gasps, but she kept moving.

A beautiful dancer. With a beautiful man for an instructor. He taught her to move with grace and power. Called her his greatest protégé. She believed him, even after he locked the door to the studio and dimmed the lights. The romantic words he whispered set her heart afire, even if the other things scared her at first.

Sarah crossed the street, her thighs chafing together. She waddled into Zip's Burgers and ordered the special. Five burgers and a tub of fries. Five-ninety-nine. The cashier tightened his lips to contain a snicker, but she didn't care. She was used to it.

A beautiful dancer. In love, until it all came crashing down. She begged him to marry her, to make things right, but he refused. He accused her of being a tramp and denied that it could be his. His sneer and flat eyes broke something inside of her. Not just her heart. Maybe her soul.

Her parents didn't believe her. They sent her away to Oregon to live with her aunt. She wept the entire trip, first out loud, then more quietly once her father's hand stung her cheek.

The baby grew within her. She ate to provide for her. She knew it would be a girl and decided to name it Cassie.

Seven months slipped by. Her mother called twice to check on her. Her father didn't.

She was headed to a doctor's appointment on the day of the collision. Without her seatbelt, she was tossed around inside the car like a pinball. The doctor told her he was sorry, but there was nothing he could do.

He said it had been a girl.

Sarah took the hamburgers and fries and found a corner booth. She began to eat, jamming in large mouthfuls and chewing with purpose.

A beautiful dancer. The weight never came off. Her eating didn't help matters. Her mother called it comfort food, but that wasn't true. There was a hole she kept trying to fill, but didn't gain any ground, no matter how much she ate. Eventually, it became a matter of habit, and maintenance.

Sarah finished the first burger in three bites and grabbed a handful of fries. They were hot and burned her lips and tongue. She chewed.

A beautiful dancer. He was still beautiful, too, when she found him. And his sneer was the same when she lifted her shirt over her head. But it didn't matter.

Nothing mattered, except that she could still move like a dancer. She still had a dancer's strength when she held his face tight against the naked skin of her belly. He struggled, but lying atop him, she had size, strength and vengeance on her side. When it was finished, she left him slack and open-mouthed on the apartment floor.

Sarah shoveled another handful of fries into her mouth and followed it with a deep suck from her milkshake. For the first time ever, the food tasted good.

Refrigerator Raid

by Kimberly Brown

Bennie Lovell could eat anything he wanted and
never gain an ounce. "It's a blessing," he'd tell his
beer-drinking buddies who looked nine months
pregnant by the time they were middle-aged.
Bennie's belly was washboard flat, regardless of how
many six-packs he put away.

Bennie loved the taste of food, especially junk food.
His wife Rita spent $250 a week on groceries, just for
the two of them.

Rita didn't have a blessed metabolism, and had
gained fifty pounds since she'd married Bennie
twenty years before. One day Rita put her foot down.
"I'll not buy another cookie. No more ice cream and
chips. You'll eat three healthy meals like everyone
else."

Bennie sulked, but it did him no good. Once Rita
made up her mind, that was it.

One night Bennie sat drinking beer with his best
buddy Clive in Clive's trailer.

"You know," Bennie said, "I could really go for some
potato chips."

Clive shrugged. "Don't got no money."

Bennie took another swig. "Been thinking."

Clive winced. Bennie thinking wasn't a good thing.

"The Westmillers up the hill have gone back to Florida for the winter."

"So?" Clive didn't like where this was going.

"So, they always keep a full pantry. 'Member when I fixed their refrigerator? They had food galore."

"You proposing we break and enter for potato chips?"

"It's not breakin' and enterin' if you got a key," Bennie said. He reached into his pocket and pulled out a key ring. "They gave me one to keep an eye on the place."

Clive's eyes narrowed. "You sure about that?"

Bennie looked away. "Well, maybe it's an extra I took while I was there. So what? Let's go."

Bennie led Clive to Bennie's beat-up truck.

"Rita'll kill you," Clive said, his voice sorrowful.

"Nah. She just don't want me spending money on food. She don't care how much I eat."

"If you get arrested, she'll kill you."

But Bennie wouldn't be persuaded. He drove up the mountain to the Westmiller place, with Clive fretting the whole way.

They stared at the huge, dark house.

"Them folks are funny," Clive said. "Always arguing and fighting. Even in public. Mrs. Westmiller went around with a black eye a while back."

Bennie shrugged. He could just about taste the feast he was going to have. "What people do in private's their own business."

They went up the stone walkway. Bennie put the key in the deadbolt, then in the door lock. "Same key fits both locks. Pretty handy, huh?"

They walked through the dark foyer to the great room. "Quite a spread," Bennie said. They made it to the kitchen and Bennie stuck his head in the pantry. He took out a jar of peanuts and a bag of cookies.

The refrigerator was a disappointment. Just a few cans of soda and a bottle of wine.

Bennie handed the wine to Clive and said, "Let's go to the basement. I saw a deep freeze there. Bet they got some burgers we can grill up and some ice cream too."

Clive shook his head, but followed Bennie to the basement door. "Can't believe we're doing this," he muttered.

"Wuss," Bennie said. He flicked on the lights and headed to the big chest freezer in the corner. He pushed open the heavy lid.

Clive came up beside him and they both stared into the chest. Bennie swallowed hard. Mrs. Westmiller's skin had a bad case of freezer burn.

"You said they fought a lot, huh?"

Clive nodded. "Guess he won."

For the first time in his life, Bennie lost his appetite.

ncident at Trouble Creek

by Gary Hoffman

"Grandpa, why do they call this Martin Road?" Kathie, his eight year old granddaughter asked.

Grandpa Baker smiled and glanced over at his two grandchildren riding in the front seat of his pickup with him. "Well, a long time ago, the man who lived at the end of this road was named Martin."

"Is that where a lot of things get names, from people?" Davy his eleven year old grandson asked.

"Lots of times, yes."

"Well, we just went over Trouble Creek. Where did that name come from? Or is it one of those stories we have to wait until we're grown up to hear? Half of what mom and dad talk about is like that," Davy said disgustedly.

"No you can hear this story. Several years ago a man named Frankie Pappas and his gang robbed several banks up in Georgia."

"Wow, is this like an old West story?" Davy asked.

"Sort of. Anyway, when the law got hot on their trail in Georgia, they took off and came down here to this part of Florida. Frankie's nickname was "Tiny." He weighed almost four hundred pounds."

"Why would they call him Tiny if he was so big?" Davy asked.

"Well, sometimes people get nicknames that really don't fit them."

"So what happened?" Davy asked.

"When they got down here, they camped out by the creek we just went over. Creek didn't have any name at the time. They got hungry and shot one of the neighbor's cows. Then they got into an argument about who would get to eat what off the cow. Tiny apparently had a fierce appetite, and he pretty much wanted the whole cow for himself."

"Nobody could eat a whole cow!"

"You're right, Davy. But they got into a fight anyway. Tiny started shooting the other gang members so he could eat it all. He killed two of them, but only wounded the other guy who got away. The wounded man walked into town for help. He was so mad at Tiny for shooting him and wanting the whole cow he went to the sheriff and told him where Tiny was hiding."

"What did the sheriff do?" Davy asked excitedly.

"Well, the sheriff never had anyone as famous as Tiny to go after, and he got pretty shook up. He started to round up a posse to help him. He just knew there was going to be a big gun battle. He was telling everyone there was going to be big trouble by the creek west of town. From then on, it just became known as Trouble Creek."

"What happened next?" Davy asked.

"By the time they got there, the sheriff had thirty men with him, all armed and ready to fight. They saw smoke from Tiny's campfire, so they spread out to make a circle around him and snuck up on him. Tiny had roasted a whole hind quarter of that cow and had managed to eat most of it. When the posse jumped out to arrest him, he was propped up against a tree sound asleep." Grandpa Baker laughed. "He was real easy to arrest and take to jail. From what I heard, he didn't even want to wake up, he was so full."

"Is that true?" Davy said.

"Every word," Grandpa Baker said. "My daddy was on that posse."

"Wow!" Davy said.

"I didn't know Grandpas had daddies," Kathie said.

"Well, I guess that is one of those stories you will have to wait until you're grown up to hear," Grandpa Baker said, as he smiled and kept on driving.

Cristofori faciem die quacunque tueris · Millesimo ccc°
Illa nempe die morte mala non morieris · xx° anno :5:

ntil Death

by BJ Bourg

Greg Newton pushed Sarah to the bed. "I'm your husband. You've got to give it to me any time I want it!"

Tears streamed down Sarah's pale face. "It's not normal to want it as much as you do! I need a break! You're hurting me!"

Greg grabbed Sarah's shirt near the collar and jerked it open. Thread ripped and buttons clattered against the walls. He pushed his right hand roughly against her left breast and smashed it between his fingers. He clutched at the front of his jeans with his left hand.

"No! Please, don't!" Sarah's chin trembled. She tried to push Greg away, but he was too strong—too hungry. He dropped onto her and ravished her body, over and over.

When Greg was done, Sarah lay still for some time. Her head throbbed. When she attempted to sit up, the pain in her gut and the burning between her legs were too great. She groaned and rolled to her side.

"You ready for another round?" Greg's breath was hot against the back of her neck. He reached around and clasped her breast.

"Please don't," she said in a faint voice, "you're hurting me."

"You should be flattered that I can't get enough of you." Greg sat up on the bed and rolled Sarah to her back. She winced as pain coursed through her body.

"Greg, we've had sex seven times a day since our marriage. I can't go any more."

"It's only been two weeks. You're already turning into the typical icebox of a wife. You promised this wouldn't happen."

"I didn't know you'd want it so much."

"Neither did I. Had I known sex was this great, I would've lost my virginity a long time ago." Greg plopped on top of Sarah and pressed his mouth against hers. His whiskers scraped at her lips and chin, causing a penetrating burn.

Sarah wept silently as Greg pleasured himself for the fifth time that day. When he rolled off, she lay panting. The pain from earlier had transcended to a hellish torture. She didn't even know she needed to urinate until she felt the burn and then the warmth on her leg.

"Jesus Christ! You wet the bed." Greg jumped to his feet and stormed into the bathroom.

Sarah took a deep, piercing breath and pulled herself to a seated position. She was fueled by the thought that this might be her only chance to escape the ravenous clutches of this man– this stranger she called her husband.

Sarah felt around on the floor until she located Greg's jeans. She reached deep into the front pocket and found his knife. With trembling hands, she opened the blade and lay back on the bed, the knife concealed beneath the blankets.

Greg returned and leaned over to jerk the sheet off the bed. As he did so, Sarah shot forward and plunged the knife deep into his throat. Greg's mouth dropped open. He clutched at his throat. Blood spurted through his fingers—

Sarah shot upright in bed and gasped. There was no pain. She let out a long sigh of relief and laughed. *I've been dreaming!* Sarah turned to Greg.

She screamed as she stared down at her husband's lifeless body. A knife was buried in his throat. She stood and cursed her insatiable desire to take the lives of the men she married. Would that thirst for blood ever be fully quenched? Sarah shook her head and slowly began to pack—for the eighth time that year.

ittle White Lies

by John M. Floyd

"Well, would you look at that," Dennis said.

Across the road, a blue Cadillac pulled into the empty gravel lot of Jimbo's Package Store and cut its lights. From his hiding place in the bushes Dennis Penzler caught a glimpse of blond hair, a jeweled bracelet.

"Melissa White," Dennis said. "Know her?"

Beside him, Pete Harrell frowned. "Citizens for Decency?"

"CFD, youth counselor, PTA president, Sunday School teacher. And rich widow. Goes to church with my mom."

They watched Ms. White climb out of her car, look around, hurry into Jimbo's.

"Got your handkerchief?"

Pete blinked. "I thought we decided not to rob—"

"Not the store." Dennis pulled a revolver. "The customer."

"But– what if she recognizes you?"

"Doesn't matter. That's the beauty of it."

"What?"

"Here," Dennis said, holding up his own handkerchief. "Help me tie this."

Five minutes later, Melissa White left the liquor store lugging a cardboard box. She crunched through the gravel–and froze.

Two men wearing white masks blocked her way. One held a pistol.

"Your purse, Madam," he said.

She stood there clutching the box to her chest, studying his eyes. "I know you. Martha Penzler's son. Dennis."

The other young man groaned.

"But you won't tell," Dennis said.

"Why not?"

"Here you are, the pure-as-snow Baptist, twenty miles from home, midnight–buying booze. Want that news to get out?"

She stared at him. "You're making a mistake, Dennis."

"Don't lie, Ms. White. I imagine you've told enough lies already. In fact you look a little wobbly tonight."

"It's not what you think."

"Course not. This is probably church business." He pointed to the closed box. "Bottles of OJ for the prayer breakfast?"

She turned to show him the words on the side: METRO MARCH OF DIMES CRUSADE.

His smile disappeared.

"Jars, not bottles," she said. "With coin slots in the top."

Dennis's shoulders sagged. "But... in this part of town—"

"Jimbo Cobb and I went to school together. All his stores bring their donations here. The drive ends tomorrow." She held out the box. "Here. You're robbing me, might as well take this too."

Dennis hesitated. Seconds dragged by.

"Your call, Dennis. But if you do it I'm reporting you."

He swallowed. "We could kill you."

"You could. Or you could leave, right now. You do, I'll forget this ever happened."

It was suddenly quiet in the parking lot. A light wind riffled Melissa's hair. Somewhere far away, a siren whined.

That seemed to make up Dennis's mind. Without another word he and his friend turned and fled.

Melissa White watched them go, then got into her car and put the box on the passenger seat. That's when the shaking started.

She trembled for a full minute. Finally she drew several deep breaths and wiped her eyes. She looked across the road at the dark woods that had swallowed her two attackers.

She knew she'd been lucky. All of them had been lucky. She had somehow kept two idiots from ruining their lives and had managed not to get herself killed or robbed in the process.

And she'd done it with one little lie. Thank God Jimbo used old boxes. She pondered that as she opened it, removed one of the six bottles, and took the first long fiery swallow.

No small thing, not getting robbed: Bourbon and Scotch, in the quantities she required, were expensive. Only Jimbo knew how broke she was.

That thought made her smile. Some of what she'd said was actually true.

They *had* gone to school together...

urtain Call

by Sunny Frazier

"Romeo" was fat.

Jerome Grout made his appearance at the Shakespeare Festival in Ashland, Oregon a scant three days before the first performance. Warren, the director, had the rest of the troupe rehearse around the leading man's absence. "Juliet" was sick of saying lines to the understudy.

"You've put on over a hundred pounds during the winter break," Warren screamed at the leading man. "You couldn't even play Falstaff! Get off my stage."

Jerome whipped out a legal document and shoved it in the director's face. "You'll just have to make adjustments. I'm under contract."

The producer had sought out Jerome after a monumental performance as Hamlet at a San Francisco dinner theater. Now he was the producer's paramour and the director was stuck with him for the summer season.

Beaten, Warren and the cast tried their best to accommodate their overweight Romeo. It wasn't easy.

47

"He eats garlic before the kissing scenes," said "Juliet."

"He passes gas in the wings," whined a stagehand.

"He never stops gorging himself," complained the caterer.

Warren caught his star stuffing food in the pockets of his tunic. The costume designer was instructed to sew them closed. Larger tights were ordered.

On opening night, Jerome made his entrance on Verona's fair streets. The audience tittered. They laughed uneasily when he fell off the trellis in the balcony scene. By the end of a lumbering sword fight with the Capulet gang, people were convulsing in their seats.

During intermission, the director circulated among the crowd, listening to their appraisals.

"It's certainly an original take on the play," commented one baffled patron.

"I've never thought of 'Romeo and Juliet' as a comedy," mused a woman between sips of Chablis. "Although, when you think about it, two kids committing suicide over love is rather silly."

"Directors aren't content to leave well enough alone," sniffed a critic. "This is the most ridiculous interpretation I've ever seen."

Incensed, Warren returned backstage. Jerome was in place at the cast's refreshment table, popping miniature cream puffs into his mouth. The director whispered an idea to the caterer, key actors and two stagehands. Heads bobbed in eager agreement.

Their leading man continued to snack between scenes. Before Act Five, Scene One, he gobbled down more pastries, missing his cue. Warren dragged him away from the goodies and pushed him onstage.

In an overly dramatic pose of the exiled Romeo, Jerome recited, "I dreamt my lady came and found me dead."

He stopped. The next line came out as a gurgle as Jerome clutched his throat. He fell to the ground, writhing. In less than a minute, it was over.

"I don't remember the death scene coming this early in the play," a woman whispered to her husband.

The troupe never missed a beat. They'd rehearsed so many hours without Jerome; it was easy to continue. They stepped artfully around his inert body until the stagehands discreetly dragged the corpse stage left.

The producer rushed backstage in a state of anguish. "What the hell happened?"

"I think he choked on a cream puff." Warren shrugged. "He crammed five of them into his mouth before his entrance."

The producer picked up a treacherous puff and crushed it in his hand. "These aren't creampuffs---

they're shrimp balls!" He turned to the caterer. "I told you, no shellfish. Jerome had allergies."

Warren winked at the caterer. It only took a tiny script change.

But the show must go on.

Demon of Gluttony

ore to Love

by Deborah Elliott-Upton

"Roy isn't half the man you are," Carlos said, chuckling.

If he could have reached the scrawny maggot, Joe would have decked him. Leaning on the table, he hefted himself upright, then shuffled to the buffet line.

Carlos danced around him like gnats on a rotting peach. "Gonna ask her out tonight, Joe? Huh? Are ya?"

Joe grunted and shoveled a fresh pile of tamales over the china until none of the white remained. If he couldn't have Delilah for himself, he'd at least bankrupt her boyfriend's restaurant. With Roy's money gone, he wouldn't be as tough a rival. Still, that white boy knew how to cook and the all-you-can-eat price was good, too.

Somehow, Joe would get Delilah alone and tell her the truth. Tonight she would see him for the man he was, not just another guy wanting her, but one who would give her his all.

Sitting at the table, Carlos babbled about needing money. Carlos always needed money, so Joe only half-listened. He kept one eye on the petite waitress and the other on his plate.

As she neared, he pasted on a grin, downed his tea and tilted the glass back and forth as a signal. "How's it going?" he asked as Delilah refilled his glass.

"Fine," she said.

"Delilah, I was wondering – " Joe began.

"Yes?"

Joe stared at his plate. "Any more tamales out yet?"

Carlos leaned back and cackled.

Delilah ignored Carlos. "Roy's bringing some out now."

"Um, thanks," Joe managed.

As she walked away, Carlos poked Joe in the ribs. "Smooth talker."After a moment, Carlos added, "Bet they bring in a lot of money. Hell, we ought to rob 'em. Be easy. Roy leaves the register alone just waiting for someone to fill their pockets. Hey, I got an idea. You get their attention. I'll grab the cash. We'll split 50/50. Deal?"

"Nah," Joe said.

"Fine, just eat 'em out of business."

Joe watched Delilah and Roy talking, their heads close together. A little too close, he thought. Shoving the remaining tamales into his mouth, he stood. "Make it fast."

Joe waddled to the buffet and piled a volcano of tamales on his plate. "Hey, Delilah. Roy," he said.

A glop of tamale sauce flooded from his plate like lava and landed on the floor. One tamale followed, then another. As he stepped forward, Joe's right shoe slid forward like he was attempting to do the splits. His body swayed from left to right and back again in a poor Stevie Wonder imitation.

The plate of tamales swerved one way, then the other. Losing his balance, Joe toppled forward in a slow-motion avalanche. Delilah stood in front of him wide-eyed. The plate teetered again. Tamales splayed across Joe's stomach and cascaded down his pants like a sluggish waterfall.

Delilah grabbed for the dish and missed. China clattered against the tiles, rolling across the foyer. Gasping, her outstretched arms tried to end Joe's momentum. A loud squish like Halloween pumpkins being smashed against the asphalt resounded in Joe's ears. He felt a leg bone snap with the impact. Someone screamed.

For a moment, he heard nothing except his lungs valiantly trying to refill with air. When he caught his breath, Joe saw what had broken his fall.

Delilah's tiny body was crushed beneath him, insulating him from the floor. Her head tilted too far back like a permanently open Pez dispenser.

Tonight, Delilah discovered Joe for the man he truly was, all 459 pounds of him. He had given her his all.

Sloth

The slothful in their pit of snakes in Hell.

prah's Smile

by Frank Zafiro

Panicked, Barbara stumbled toward her chair.

The opening music for Oprah blared out of the ancient TV set. The bass tones vibrated through the small speaker, but she refused to turn it down. There was no remote control for the TV, so once she turned it on, everything was locked in. No way was she going from couch to TV and back every sixty minutes.

Bad enough that she almost missed the introduction to the program to use the bathroom. Then the toilet paper ran out. The last roll wasn't under the sink but in the hall closet. She ran an indoor marathon just to make it back in time to hear the clapping diminish as Oprah introduced the show.

It would be a one-on-one interview, she saw. With who? Oprah dropped a few hints, but Barbara didn't want to waste the effort to figure it out. *Just tell me.*

Her hand snaked down to the cooler next to her chair. She kept her eyes glued to the set while she rummaged around. Her expert fingers identified the food item by the size, shape and the texture of the packaging. Oprah wasn't finished dropping clues about her guest before Barbara realized there was an extra Ding-Dong.

She smiled and pulled it from the cooler. She glanced at the empty wrappers on the table in front of her. Six there already. That meant Hank brought her an extra one today. She unwrapped it and devoured it in two bites. It tasted funny. Stale, maybe.

Oprah smiled on TV, opened her arms expansively and revealed her mystery guest. Barbara looked up long enough to watch a ridiculously thin redhead walk from backstage and greet Oprah. The two sat down to chat.

Barbara frowned. She didn't even *like* this actress or her movies. Not that she'd been to the theater in ages, but Hank occasionally brought her DVDs. It was too much work to deal with the player, but he'd put one in before he left. That was great if the movie was a good one, but that was rare. Usually it was terrible and she could hardly stand sitting in her chair and watching it seven or eight times until he came back.

The room seemed to wobble, so she leaned her head back and closed her eyes. She was still sweating from her earlier exertion. Hank should buy her a new TV. It was only fair. He got all the breaks in this life, so he owed her a little bit, didn't he?

Instead, she got resentment. Only three days ago, he laid into her about doing nothing with her life. She just sat around and ate and watched TV, he yelled. She was a burden. It was like she was already dead.

Easy for him to say. Her brother had all the luck. Wife, job, a life. What did she have? She scowled. She didn't have a goddamn remote, that's what. And nothing to do but sit and wait for a full hour until Oprah ended.

Nobody understood. She *tried*, she really did, but she was just so tired all the time. And her disability check provided enough to get by, as long as Hank kept up his end and brought the food like he was supposed to.

Barbara tried to swallow and discovered she couldn't. Her tongue was thick and covered with paste. She took a deep, croaking breath. Her pulse pounded in her temples.

She coughed and it turned into a gag.

A red darkness appeared at the corners of her vision. Her eyes bulged. Oprah smiled.

uke Knowles:
Professional Student

by Gary Hoffman

"And how many years have you been in college now?" Luke's father asked him.

"I really don't know."

"You really don't know," his father said in a mocking tone. "Well, I know! Nine years! When are you gonna get out in the real world and get a job?"

"I'm just not sure what I want to do yet."

"I know the answer to that one, too. Nothin'! That's what you want to do. Nothin'!" Ed Knowles paused. "God, I wish your mother were still alive to help me with this."

"I don't think Mom would object if I stayed in college until I figured out what I wanted to do."

Ed sighed. "You're probably right there. She spoiled you rotten!"

Luke took a deep breath. He clenched and unclenched his fists. "You know you were never around when I was growing up. You were always working. That what you want me to become? You?"

"Hey, I worked to give you and your mother a good life. You both had everything you ever wanted."

"Except you."

"Well, I wasn't sittin' around on my lazy butt lettin' someone support me!" Ed got up from his deck chair on the stern of his yacht named *Maggie*, in honor of his dead wife. He walked over to the bar and made another Scotch on the rocks.

"So you think that's what I'm doing? Letting you support me? Good going, old man. It only took you nine years to figure that out! Just as soon as you're gone, I'll have everything and won't have to work a day for the rest of my life."

Ed walked over to where Luke was standing by the railing. He pushed his finger in Luke's chest. "Yes, that's exactly what I think!"

Luke slapped his hand away. "Don't ever touch me! Ever!"

Ed crowded up against Luke to where he was right in his face. "And just what the hell are you gonna do about it?" His evening of drinking was starting to talk now.

Luke shoved him away. Ed stumbled backwards, but caught himself on a deck chair before he fell. He dropped his glass, and it shattered on the deck. He got his balance back and lunged at Luke. Luke stepped to the side and pushed his father on the back as he ran by. Ed slipped on the deck and made a grab for the railing, but missed. He fell off the yacht and into the waters of Bay Brook Marina. Luke turned and looked down into the clear water.

Luke knew his father couldn't swim. He saw him just a few feet below the surface. His eyes were open, and he was struggling to reach the surface, but losing the battle. Bubbles were coming from his nose and mouth. Luke looked around to make sure no one was witnessing this scene. When he looked back down, his father was gone.

Luke walked over the bar and poured a glass of bourbon. He raised it up in a mock toast. "To the good life! I finally outlasted the old bastard!"

lovenly Secrets

by Sunny Frazier

"Are you sure Lisa's going to be out of the house tonight?"

Vicky looked impatiently at Brit. "It's her anniversary. Don's taking them out for sushi."

"She hates sushi," Brit pointed out.

"Like everything else, Don made the decision. What she likes doesn't matter," said Vicky.

After checking several flowerpots, Kimberly found a spare key. "Let's do it."

They entered the darkened house and turned on their flashlights.

"What a pig sty!"

Papers were stacked on the surfaces of tables and chairs. Books teetered on bookshelves, defying the laws of gravity. Newspapers filled every corner. Dust bunnies scampered across the floor.

"I can't believe Lisa lives like this," Brit said.

Kimberly agreed. "She always looks so pristine in public. Never a run in her nylons."

"It's Don's fault. After a decade of cleaning up after him, she just gave up." Vicky pulled a lawn bag from a roll.

"This explains why we were never invited to her house to play cards." Brit slipped a paper face mask over her nose and mouth.

Kimberly entered the kitchen. Dishes were stacked in the sink. She pulled on a pair of yellow rubber gloves and went to work.

They'd uncovered Lisa's secret when Vicky dropped by one afternoon. Lisa only opened the door a crack, but Vicky saw the disaster. She'd made a full report to her friends.

The three women weren't clean queens, although there was competition to see who bought the latest cleaning products. They spent their free time scouring grocery shelves for the most effective disinfectants, the newest incarnation of air fresheners, advances in furniture polish. Their homes gleamed. Their closets were an ode to organization.

In an hour and forty-three minutes, they were done. They took a minute to admire their handiwork. Brit suggested they *feng shui* the living room and started to move the couch. The others vetoed the plan.

"Let's take a peek at the other rooms," Kimberly said.

"No time," Vicky answered.

But Kimberly headed down the hall anyway. She opened a door and reeled back. "You need to see this."

It was an office decorated for a man's taste. Everything was immaculate. The only mess was on the desk where Don's bloody head rested. A bust of Plato on the floor was covered with blood.

"We're going to be suspects," Brit wailed.

"How will they know?" said Vicky. "We didn't leave fingerprints." White cotton gloves covered their hands, except for Kimberly. She still had on rubber ones.

When Lisa drove up to her house, two police cars were parked in the front.

"Is there a problem, officers?" She shielded her eyes from the flashing blue and red lights.

"We received a call of a burglary in progress, ma'am."

Lisa's hand shook as she handed over her house keys. The two officers did a sweep of the house.

"We have a Code 187 at the scene," a young policeman spoke into a radio clipped on his shoulder strap. The other gently guided Lisa to Don's office.

"Do you know this man?" he asked.

But Lisa wasn't interested in identifying the body. She turned and walked back to the living room. It looked like something out of *Home Beautiful*. The policeman asked again.

"It's my husband, Don," Lisa said absently.

"Ma'am, are you okay?"

"I'm fine. Everything's perfect." Lisa had a serene smile on her face.

The words "51-50" passed between the homicide detectives, code word for crazy.

Lisa glowed with happiness all the way to the mental ward. It was all so neatly done.

So tidy.

atnapping

by John M. Floyd

"S.P. what?"

"S.P.C.A.T.H.," The bartender said. "That's who you need. They're in the phone book."

Charlie Davis sighed and took a sip of beer. It was a rainy afternoon, he was the only customer, and his mood was as dark as this end of the bar.

"You mean, like, S.P.C.A.?" he said. "The animal rights group?"

"No, no. Different bunch." The bartender picked up a glass the size of his thumb and polished it with a dishcloth. "Look. You said your wife's cat's running you crazy, right? Probably scratching up the furniture, hair all over the place, crawling on you while you watch TV?"

Charlie nodded sadly. "That, and more."

"Then there's your answer. S.P.C.A.T.H. Ask Tom Pender, or Joe Sims. They're in here last week, same problem. One phone call, everything's taken care of."

Charlie started to reply, then paused. He had heard something--a roaring, whooshing noise. Probably something out in the street.

"I still don't follow you," he said to the bartender. "What is this S.P.C.--"

"A.T.H. Society for the Prevention of Cats Around The House."

"What?!"

"It's a service. One call, they come in, cat's gone."

Charlie stared in disbelief. "You mean, they're like... hit men?"

"Prevention, not extermination. They nap 'em. Cart 'em off to Mexico, I heard." The bartender put the shotglass down behind the counter and slung the dishtowel over one shoulder. "Want another beer?"

"Why Mexico?"

"Maybe husbands down there like cats. Who knows?"

"That's incredible," Charlie said, shaking his head. "Professional catnappers." He turned and squinted at the front window. The noise he had heard was growing louder.

He drummed his fingers on the bar, thinking. Of one thing he was certain: something had to be done, either about the cat or--

"Don't suppose there's an S.P.W.A.T.H., is there?" he said, smiling. "Wives instead of cats?"

The bartender didn't smile. "In addition to," he said, lowering his voice.

"What?"

"The cat folks are in the phone book. The other group--let's just say they're a little more secretive. But one call can arrange both."

"You're serious?"

"Double your pleasure. Fee's higher, though."

Charlie just sat there, his mouth hanging open. This was almost too much to absorb. Finally he said, "Think the wives get shipped off to Mexico too?"

"Could be. They'd want to be with the cats."

"How much is the fee, you think? For both?"

"Not bad, I'm told," the bartender said. "You say so, they even supply you a dog in return."

"A dog?"

"Sims got a black Lab. Takes him fishing."

"Hmm." This was sounding better and better. Charlie looked around in the gloom. The whooshing noise had grown so loud it was making his head hurt. "Got a phone book I could use?"

"Sure." The bartender reached behind him, turned, and–

THUMP! The heavy book hit Charlie in the chest.

He coughed, then sputtered, "What'd you throw it for?"

"I didn't throw it, I dropped it," his wife said. "You told me you'd fix the toaster, there it is. Fix it. And get up so I can vacuum the cushions."

Charlie blinked. He was sprawled on his living-room sofa, the vacuum cleaner roaring in his ear. Still half asleep and holding the toaster, he rose, stumbled to his recliner, started to sit down–and was stopped by his wife's shrill voice.

"Not there!" she said. "Sit at the table."

"The table? Why?"

"Why do you think?" She pointed to his chair. "You almost sat on the cat."

asy Come, Easy Go

by Deborah Elliott-Upton

"This is my favorite game," the kid said.

"Yeah, kid, a game," George answered.

"Don't make it so easy this time. My sister ties me up every day and I always get out."

"Sure. Now pipe down while I make this call." George punched the numbers on the throwaway cell and waited for the kid's parents to answer. His attention wavered back to his charge who wriggled like an eel. He didn't really hear the recorded message, but hung up before the beep. No need putting his voice on a recorder for some wiseacre cop to identify.

The heavyset man shifted his weight making the bedsprings sag even more. He stared at the average-looking six-year-old. *Except he's heir to a fortune*, he thought.

George didn't know what to do with the pint-sized Houdini. The kid already wriggled out of the ropes three times. This wasn't easy. George liked easy.

But Big Mike managed to find him *too* easily. Those TV ads lied. Sometimes what happens in Vegas follows you home. Big Mike's reach certainly made it to Louisville and George without much trouble. Thinking an easy way to pay off Big Mike was a quick grab of the boy, collect the cash from the parents and send the kid packing while heading to Reno sounded easy enough.

Perspiration trickled down George's neck. The clown makeup worked as a disguise, but he wished the weather cooperated because he wasn't going to reapply. August in Kentucky was hell. George hadn't spent too much time on the plan or even deciding which kid to snatch. Too much trouble. He'd simply picked the first kid outside playing on the block known as Millionaire Row. The kid had come willingly, anxious to traipse after the clown who had balloons in his van.

Getting the phone number was easy, too. Parents pounded such information in a child's head at early ages these days. They must have forgotten the "Don't talk to Strangers" spiel.

George hit redial, but the line was busy. *What kind of millionaire didn't have call waiting?*

The kid cackled, an ear-splitting laugh that hurt George's ears. When he looked, the kid had once again released himself from the ropes.

"I don't want to play that game anymore," he said. "I'm bored. What video games do you have?"

"NASCAR racing."

"Play with me," the kid ordered.

"I'm tired," George said. "I'll watch."

George popped the cartridge into his PS2. For a few minutes he watched as the kid chose the red '56 Thunderbird. George's favorite, too. He leaned back on the bed and thought about Big Mike's goons. They weren't the type to listen to reason and to tell the truth, George was damn tired of trying to think of reasons anyway. Better to pay them and get it over.

He tried the phone again, but the line still buzzed annoyingly. The game's noise droned in the background, the kid totally entranced with the car race through the Italian hillside.

Eyes closed, George laid the phone next to him and imagined an air-conditioned Vegas casino, yanking one-armed bandits and grabbing free drinks from the hottie cocktail waitresses.

Something hard jabbed George's rib cage. *Damn kid.* He scrunched one eye open and saw blue.

"Get up," the uniformed cop barked.

"Where's the —"

"Kid called his folks when you fell asleep. He read the address off your mail so we could pick him up. On your feet. You're in big trouble."

George did as he was told. It was easier in the long run and he liked easy better than anything.

An Indolent Heart

By BJ Bourg

Lydia Becker stared down at Tom. He was squeezed into his recliner, beer in one hand, remote in the other. His T-shirt was pulled up, exposing a grotesque blimp of a belly.

"Why don't you go cut the grass?" Lydia asked.

"You know I'm disabled."

"Laziness ain't a disability."

"Why don't you get off my ass?"

"Why don't *you* get off your ass? I do everything around here. All you do is sit in that damn chair and watch TV. I'm getting tired of this shit!"

"Move out. Oh, wait a minute, you can't!" Tom's belly jiggled with laughter. "If you don't want to go to prison, shut the fuck up and get your ass to work."

Tears welled in Lydia's eyes. She swallowed the flood of emotion that stirred deep within her and thought back to a time when Tom wasn't so lazy. Back before he found the diary.

"You're an asshole," Lydia whispered. "I hope your heart gets as lazy as you."

Tom waved his hand in a dismissive manner. "Pick up a six pack of Budweiser on your way home from work."

Lydia grunted and stormed out the door. She made the familiar drive to work and arrived ten minutes late. Her best friend Janice was seated in the kitchen.

"Sorry I'm late," Lydia muttered.

"Asshole's at it again?"

"Lazier and meaner than ever."

"I say put him where Danny is."

"I can't. I don't know where he hid my diary."

Janice rubbed the prickly hairs on her chin. "I still can't believe you wrote that in your diary."

"I write everything in my diary."

"But a murder confession?"

"Look, I'll find it."

"At least you didn't write where we hid the body."

Lydia was silent.

"You've got to be shitting me!"

"I'll find the damn thing, and then we'll poison him, too."

Janice shook her head. "This is the last husband I'll help you bury. After that, you're on your own."

When Lydia's shift was over, she drove home. The blank expression on her face became curious as flashing lights came into view. She slipped out of her car and ducked under the crime scene tape that surrounded her house. A uniformed cop stopped her. There were two stripes on each of his shoulders.

"What's going on?" Lydia demanded.

"Are you Mrs. Becker?"

"Yes. What–?" Lydia gasped when she saw four medics struggling to squeeze a gurney through the front door. A white sheet was draped over the large body strapped to the gurney. A hand hung down past the sheet and she recognized Tom's wedding ring.

The officer touched Lydia's shoulder. "Ma'am, I'm sorry."

"But, what happened?"

"Coroner says it looks like a massive coronary."

"Serves him right," Lydia muttered.

"What's that?"

"Nothing. It's just that he was very lazy. I always told him his heart would get too tired to beat some day."

"Sergeant," a voice called from inside the house. "Get in here!"

The sergeant turned and walked briskly into the house. Lydia followed him into the living room. Another officer stood over Tom's recliner. He turned and handed the sergeant something. "Found this under the body."

Lydia gasped. *Lazy bastard's been sitting on it the whole while!*

The Sergeant thumbed through the diary and paused for a moment to read a marked page. When he was done, he slowly closed it and nodded to the officer. "Get some shovels and start digging in the back yard by the tool shed." He turned to face Lydia. "Ma'am, you have the right to remain silent..."

NWS News at Six

By Kimberly Brown

Nadine Baxter settled into her favorite spot on the sofa and flicked on the television. She heard Tommy's footsteps in the hallway but didn't look up. He stood beside the couch and she could feel his tight-lipped disapproval.

Finally he moved a pile of clothes from the coffee table and sat facing her. "I don't think I'll be home for dinner."

Nadine shrugged. "Whatever." She craned her neck to see the television screen. At least she wouldn't have to listen to him bitch and moan about the house. What had she done all day? Why weren't the dishes done? Why wasn't the bed made?

Tommy left without another word. Nadine watched her morning news shows, then Oprah. Finally, at noon the news came on again.

"I'll show him I don't just sit around all day," Nadine muttered to herself. She went to the sink and glared at the dishes Tommy had left last night. They had an agreement that if he cooked, she'd clean up, but she knew he purposely dirtied as many dishes as he could. She hated doing dishes, almost more than she hated any other housework. Such drudgery was beneath someone who'd completed almost a year of college. True, the college had been years ago, but still...

Nadine turned on the little television in the kitchen. She began to put the dishes in the dishwasher without rinsing them. So what if they didn't get clean? That'd teach Tommy to do them himself. As she picked up the big knife he'd used to slice raw chicken, the blonde news-bimbo, Jeanette, launched into the top news story.

"This afternoon a woman allegedly murdered her husband and her husband's mistress," Jeanette said with relish. "Witnesses at the scene say the woman, Nadine Baxter, claims her husband brought his mistress home with him, to tell his wife he wanted a divorce."

Nadine stared at the small screen, her mouth open. Had the bimbo said her name?

"The police aren't releasing any details, but witnesses say Nadine Baxter apparently flew into a rage and stabbed her husband and his girlfriend multiple times with a butcher knife." Jeanette's eyes were wide. Nadine stared at the knife clutched in her white-knuckled hand.

"The dead man's name is Thomas Baxter, but the name of the woman is not being released until family is notified."

The show cut to the handsome roving reporter interviewing Nadine's neighbor, Edna Winslow. "I saw her chase the woman out into the yard and stab her," Edna said in awe. "Guess she'd already killed Tommy. That Nadine is a strange one."

Jeanette had on her frozen Barbie-doll smile when the camera cut back to her. "WNWS News at Six will return after these messages."

News at six! Nadine turned to look at the clock above the stove. It was only 12:20. That should have been the noon news, not six o'clock. A hot fever of blood rushed to her face and pounded behind her eyes. Her fingers held the knife in a death grip.

Just then, she heard the kitchen door creak open. "Nadine," Tommy said. A woman Nadine recognized as one of Tommy's coworkers stood behind him, as if trying to hide. "We need to talk for a minute, okay?"

Nadine held the knife down at her side. She could feel it dripping water on her bare feet.

The door slammed shut. "Nadine," Tommy said, "Alicia and I have to tell you something." Tommy reached behind his back and took the woman's hand.

Nadine clutched the knife. She wondered if the news reporter would really be that handsome in person.

Greed

The greedy being boiled alive in oil in Hell.

oney For Nothing

by Deborah Elliott-Upton

"Tahiti's perfect for a honeymoon," Dan said. "Too bad I can't take you."

"Honeymoon?"

"Mine and Anna's. Darling, I love *you*, but a guy's gotta take care of himself. Don't worry, there's a nice divorce settlement in the future. The pre-nup's a joke."

"But, Dan–"

"We'll be together again. Only, with plenty of money." He groaned as he kissed Gina hard. "Oh, baby, I'll miss you."

"When will I see you?"

"After the divorce. I need that money."

***

The next seven months were obliterated by routine. As the perfect husband, Dan watched Anna swallow a myriad of pills for her heart, blood pressure and whatever ailment hypochondria dictated from her personal supplier, the pharmacies she owned all over town. No one said, "No," to such an influential boss.

After two months, Dan realized the pre-nup wasn't paltry, but in comparison to her holdings, it really was a joke. On him.

Dan's casual mention of new supplements from Mexico was all it took to induce his bride to increase her medications. He made sure one of the servants ordered the drugs at her personal request.

Thoughts of Gina eventually faded from his daydreams and never worrying about money again took precedence. He grew comfortable in his new lifestyle and barely remembered days of no cab fare, late payments or missed meals.

He was golfing when notified of Anna's death. An autopsy was performed with no objections from the grieving husband.

"She must have gotten confused and taken too many pills," the doctor said. "She was quite inebriated."

Dan broke into sobs. "I begged her to stop drinking."

A tasteful funeral followed. "Anna wouldn't like anything opulent," Dan told her friends. Anna's will stipulated substantial properties to the sparse family left, so none contested her husband's inheritance.

When Gina phoned, he steeled himself, then relaxed. She knew the drill. Anna's servants weren't deaf or stupid. Suspicions were not to be aroused in any circumstances. "So nice of you to call, Miss Williams. Anna was fond of the artwork she'd commissioned from you."

"Her sculpture's finished. Shall I bring it over?"

"No. Meet me at Umberto's at noon."

***

Dan approached her table slowly. He imagined the rumor mill kicking into gear, going from a low hum to a roar as he dined with a beautiful woman. Only, Gina didn't resemble the image tickling his memory. He'd fantasized about her million dollar legs. In reality, she looked now more like a hundred-dollar hooker.

"Miss Williams," he said a bit too loud. "Good of you to come."

When she stood, her napkin dropped to the floor. They dove for it simultaneously, their hands brushing.

"Missed me?" she asked.

"Sure," he answered.

"When do I get you back?"

"Soon."

"How'd you do it?"

"Please. Sit," he said, then whispered. "Extra pills here and there washed down with martinis. I knew that would do her in and the autopsy couldn't nail me. Now the money's mine."

"Yours?"

"Ours," he corrected. *Damn. She's gotta go.*

A shadow fell over the table.

"A bottle of Cristal," Dan ordered.

"Hmmph! More like bread and water." The detective twisted Dan's arm behind his back. "Daniel Munson, you're under arrest for the murder of your wife, Anna Parks Munson."

"How do I get this wire off?" Gina asked innocently.

"Gina! Why?" Dan asked.

She smiled. "Inheritance brings out greed in everyone. The family offered a reward for information. Seems murderers can't be beneficiaries and a girl's gotta look out for herself. I need the money."

allen Comrades

by Sunny Frazier

Fresno is a deceptively large city: half a million people spread out over acres of former cotton fields, grapevines and fig orchards. I was only looking for one man: Sergeant Edmond Mercer.

Palms led down the long driveway, hedges cropped closer than GI haircuts fronted the house. His closest neighbors were two miles away. I'd checked it with the odometer of my rental.

I should have called first, but Mercer wouldn't slam the door in my face. War makes you brothers. A tour in Iraq makes you blood.

Over a six-pack, we became two world-weary soldiers reminiscing about the past eighteen months.

"I was glad to rotate out of that sandpit," said Mercer. "Fresno gets hot, but not like Kirkuk. How did the unit hold together after I left?"

"We lost Janski, Phillips and Lopez. Road bomb. Took out their Humvee."

He lifted his bottle. "A toast to good men and a bad war."

I took a chug. "Funny thing about our vehicles. They didn't seem to hold up as well as Bravo Company's."

Mercer shook his head. "Motor pool was in good shape when I left. The guy that replaced me must have let it go to shit."

He walked me out to the patio to admire his new swimming pool.

"Nice digs."

He smirked. "Not bad."

"You did good on a sergeants' salary."

"I saved some while I was over there. And my wife has a part-time job."

"At the copy center."

Mercer looked at me, baffled. "Yeah, that's right."

"Hey," I said, changing the subject. "Do you remember the care package my mom sent me?

"Hell yes. Best oatmeal cookies I ever ate, even though it was granola when it arrived."

"Did I show you the gadget that came with the cookies?" I pulled out a palm-size tape recorder. "Mom asked me to make tapes because she wanted to hear my voice and let me get things off my chest."

Mercer grunted. "It's good to talk. My dad never talked about 'Nam. He never talked much at all after he came home."

"Guilt?"

"Maybe. I never asked."

"How about you?"

88

He shook his head. "Nope. I don't regret killing ragheads and I don't have trouble sleeping at night."

"Maybe you should."

I held up the recorder. "The beauty of this thing is that it's voice activated. Saves on batteries. Put it down anywhere and it picks up conversations."

"Nice feature," Mercer said warily

I pressed play.

"I got good plates." A ping of steel. "Give you ten for $2,000 American."

The clear sound of his voice made Mercer jump. "What the hell?"

I pushed pause. "I recorded plenty of your black market deals on tape. Did you know it was a crime to scam the government?"

"We all took a little cream off the top."

"You sold armor plate off the chassis of the Hummers. Janski, Phillips and Lopez died for your greed."

"What do you plan to do with the tapes?"

"My conscience says I should send them to D.C. and let Uncle Sam come after your ass."

"Are you blackmailing me?"

"Not everyone's like you. I don't want to make money off this war. Revenge – that's a different story."

I pulled out my father's old service pistol, a .45.

"You'll never get away with it."

"Sure, I will. I'm heading back to Iraq to finish my tour of duty."

"Your prints are all over the house."

"All I've touched are a few beer bottles. I'm taking the empties with me."

I shot him three times. Once for each of my buddies.

Let them hunt me down in Baghdad.

or Love or Money

by Kimberly Brown

Brent McComb hunched over his keyboard. Around him, coworkers chatted about where they were going after work, but Brent ignored them. Except Monica. Her voice stood out, light and sweet.

The software company Brent worked for, ComCo, had won the prize--the contract to write a program handing out money to hurricane victims. His bosses had bid six programmers working two months to get the program finished. But, as usual, it fell in Brent's lap.

Brent, the code-monkey. The only one who knew the difference between a programming language and his own butt. Everyone else did paperwork for the project reviews and congratulated themselves on how good the presentations looked, while he did the real work.

The next time Brent looked up, the office was quiet. He'd been so lost in the code, making the ones and zeroes do his bidding, he hadn't noticed everyone leaving. He stood and stretched, rubbed his eyes, then sat back down. Now was the time to plant his special little bug. The code had been reviewed with the customer in-depth, as if the FEMA idiots had known what they were looking at. It'd go through another review before being released, but Brent knew it'd just be cursory. These people were in a hurry.

With a few strokes of his keyboard, Brent added his hidden module. He compiled and ran the program with his test data and sat back with a sigh when it ran cleanly.

With his program, every time FEMA made a payment to a hurricane victim, three dollars and three cents would be drawn off into a special account. He'd thought hard about the amount. Three dollars wasn't enough to alarm anyone. The three cents was to throw the math off. Mainly the amount was small enough to squash the guilt. It would add up quickly though.

His bug would be discovered eventually. But not before he was a millionaire, soaking in the sun – somewhere. Geography had never been Brent's strong suit. He'd always gone for math and science, and once he'd discovered computers, he'd flunked out of everything else in school. So he didn't have a degree, while his useless coworkers were overpaid because they did. But he'd find an island and a beautiful girl and one of those fruity drinks, and let these idiots do their own code.

Funny, in his fantasy the girl always looked like Monica. He knew most of the guys in the office didn't think she was anything special – brown hair, not model-thin, not flashy. But her smile was something else. In his fantasy, she was always smiling at him.

"Brent?"

Brent jumped up, trying to hide the computer screen.

"Are you okay?" Monica's voice was full of concern. "You look, well, strange."

Brent shook his head and squeaked, "No. I mean, I'm fine."

"I just wanted to invite you. You know, out with the group," Monica stammered.

"Out? Me?"

Monica looked down and Brent admired her shining brown hair. "We know you're doing most of the work. Without you, this project would fail. We want you to celebrate with us. Be our guest of honor."

Brent licked his lips. He glanced at his computer, then at Monica. He thought of the money. He could have millions.

Then she did it. She smiled at him.

Brent straightened his shoulders and tried to smooth wrinkles from his shirt. "Sure. I'd love to go. Give me five minutes to fix this bug I found, okay?"

"Bug?" Her eyes widened.

"It's nothing. Just a test module I need to take out." Who needed millions of dollars when Monica smiled at you?

ail Money

by BJ Bourg

"Ben, you've got to get me out!" Teri's hazel eyes were wide. "There're murderers in here. And the guards want to strip search me."

"How much is your bond?"

"$15,000.00."

My jaw dropped. "Are you shitting me? For drunk driving?"

Teri lowered her head. "The lady I hit died."

"But fifteen grand? *Jesus Christ!*"

"Just please get the money and get me out of here!"

"Where am I supposed to get that kind of money?"

"Our savings account."

"I can't touch that money."

"What? We've got two hundred thousand dollars--"

"Two hundred seventy-eight. But that's our life's savings. We can't touch it."

"Ben, did you hear what I said? You see that guard behind me?"

I looked past Teri at a heavyset guard with a wrinkled uniform. He leaned against the wall and stared at Teri with hungry eyes.

"What about him?"

"If you don't get me out of here, that man's going to take my clothes off, make me bend over, and he's going to spread my butt cheeks to search for drugs."

"But you don't do drugs."

"That's not the point! He already rubbed my breasts and my crotch with his filthy hands, searching for weapons..." Teri's bottom lip quivered. "Only, he wasn't searching! I feel so violated! Please, get the money!"

I shook my head. "We have to save for our future."

"God damn it! I thought you were over that sickness!"

"It's not a sickness. It's being responsible."

Teri's eyes narrowed. "Get the fucking money and get me out of here or we're *through!*"

The guard walked over and stared down at Teri. "Is there a problem?" He asked, his eyes straying to Teri's captive breasts that stretched the fabric of her shirt.

Teri crossed her arms and stared deep into my eyes. Tears streamed down her face. "Please get me out!"

***

I knew exactly where to go for the money. My dad always kept a few thousand dollars in his office. When I arrived at Global Industries, I rushed past the secretary and into Dad's office.

"Ben, your dad's not–"

I slammed the door shut behind me and scanned the plush office. The wall safe was still behind his desk. I opened the top desk drawer and smiled when I saw the combination burned into the wood. *Old habits die hard!*

I dialed in the combination and gasped when I opened the safe. There were five stacks of $100 bills. I grabbed them and checked the labels. *Twenty-thousand dollars!* I stuffed the money into the front of my pants. I had just shut the safe when the secretary burst through the door.

"Ben! I just spoke to your father. He said if you don't leave immediately to call the police."

"I'm going." I hurried to the parking lot and sped off in my car.

I was two blocks from the jail when I spotted Liberty Bank. I gripped the steering wheel with sweaty hands. My heart pounded in my chest. I only needed fifteen grand for my wife's bond. If I deposited the extra five thousand into my account, I'd have $283,000.00 put away for my future. I turned abruptly into the bank parking lot and went inside to make the deposit.

Within ten minutes I was back in my car. I stared down at my deposit receipt. The new balance read:

$298,000.00. I smiled and tucked the receipt into my shirt pocket. I looked up and sighed.

Now where in the hell am I gonna get $15,000.00 to get Teri out of jail?

Demon of Greed leading a treasure-seeking fool

our for Dinner

by John M. Floyd

The kitchen phone rang just as Carolyn Hendon
finished peeling the potatoes.

"Mrs. Hendon?" a male voice said.

"That's right."

"Mrs. Gerald J. Hendon?"

"Yes. Who's this?"

"Listen closely, Mrs. Hendon. I'm at a phone booth
near your home." A short pause. "Your husband's
here too, in his car. My partner's holding a gun to his
head."

Carolyn Hendon felt her stomach tighten.

"Mrs. Hendon?"

She swallowed. "Why should I believe you?"

"Because I gave you his name."

"You can get a name from the phone book," she said.
"A number, too."

"The phone number came from his key-ring."

"Look, I'm not convinced–"

98

"Hold on," the voice said. She heard the squeak of a sliding door, the rumble of traffic. "Green '04 Jaguar, license GJH2. Ring any bells?"

The line went quiet.

"Nice car. Be a shame to bloody the seats."

"What do you want?" she asked.

"Five hundred grand. Preferably in cash, but its equivalent in diamond jewelry would do nicely."

"What makes you think—"

"I read the papers. I know your husband's position."

A silence passed.

"Enough talking, Mrs. Hendon. Half a million. Deliver it tonight, alone, to a mailbox at 2105 Grant Road, Bridgeport."

"And what if I don't?"

"Then we'll kill him."

Another silence.

"Let me speak to him," she said.

"He's still groggy. Bump on his head, you know. Besides, I'm outside. That'd be risky."

"Then it's no deal."

"What?"

"You heard me."

The voice was lower now. "I told you we'd kill him, Mrs. Hendon. I'm not bluffing."

"Kill him, then," she said, and hung up.

She stared at the phone awhile, then sighed. "Guess it takes all kinds," she murmured.

She wiped her wet hands on a dishtowel and plugged in the mixer. Behind her, her husband Gerald appeared in the kitchen doorway. "Mom wants to know if she can help, honey," he said.

"She can help by talking to your Aunt Libby, so I won't have to. You get the wine I asked for?"

"Done." He wandered in and leaned against the counter, watching her whip potatoes. "Who was that on the phone?"

"Crank call." She'd already decided not to worry him. She flashed him a tired smile. "How about setting the table?"

"Ah. A job I can handle."

She studied him as he opened the cabinet door. "Gerald," she said, "how long since you've seen your old college buddy, the one who liked practical jokes? Baggins?"

"Bagley. Six months or so, I guess."

She turned back to her work. "Did you have the Jag then?"

"Took him to the airport in it when he left. Why?"

"And what about your license plate? The personalized one."

He stopped and looked at her. "I had that too. What's this about, Carolyn? What're you thinking?"

She switched the mixer off and tapped the blades against the bowl's rim. "I'm thinking you shouldn't park the Jag out back any more when the garage door's open, Gerald. Anybody who passes by and sees your car gone from the driveway, like now, would think you're not home." She shrugged. "Who knows, it could be dangerous for me and the kids."

He frowned. "Maybe you're right." The sound of voices from the other room interrupted them, and he continued stacking dinner plates. "But you're wrong about one thing, honey. It's not parked out back, at the moment."

She turned and stared at him. "What?"

"Dad took it down to the corner to get the wine," he said. "In fact, he should've been back by now..."

ead Time

by Frank Zafiro

He grunted in irritation and tossed the lottery scratch ticket to the floorboard. It fluttered down and landed next to nineteen others.

Goddamn tax on the stupid, and I keep paying it.

The coffee in his Styrofoam cup was cold, but he drank it anyway. Had to stay awake. Important work to do.He stared down at the numbers on his paycheck stub in disbelief. Three thousand two hundred forty dollars and sixty-one cents.

For one week.

He'd cashed it, for sure. But there was no way.

Kathy, the payroll bitch, must have screwed up. If you moved the decimal point over one spot, you got three hundred twenty-four dollars.

That was more like it. Yeah, that was the shit pay he normally got.

It was a mistake. Had to be.

But it wasn't his mistake, and there was no way he was going to suffer for it.

Because that is what would happen. Kathy was a snooty little piece who had turned her nose up at him when all he had asked was if she wanted to get some coffee or maybe see a movie sometime, but she wasn't stupid. Monday would roll around and she would do her audit and she'd see that there was a huge mistake and then *her* mistake would suddenly become *his* problem.

Story of my life.

Fuck that. He was quitting. He'd head down to Texas and see if his cousin could get him a job on an oil rig or something. He just needed a little lead time. Some delay in discovering the mistake, so that he could get out of town and disappear.

He reached down and felt the wad of cash in his pocket. It was more money than he'd ever held before.

A pair of headlights appeared at the end of the block and he hunched down in his seat. The engine had the high-pitched whine of a Geo Metro and when the familiar red vehicle passed him and pulled in front of the small, two-bedroom home half a block away, he smiled.

Everyone would be so sad. They wouldn't get to the books for days, maybe weeks.

"*How do you like me now?*" he hummed under his breath, as he watched her get out of her car. She wore a sweatshirt and shorts and looked like she'd just come from the gym. She locked the car and made her way up the walk.

He touched the wad of cash again, then hefted the small .22 caliber pistol in his hand and slipped it into his jacket pocket.

It was her mistake. *Why should he pay for it?*

He opened the car door and got out.

Martin Luther After Defeating Satan

light 249

by Gary Hoffman

"I'm tellin' ya, baby, this is gonna be great! This is the easiest way I ever thought of to hit 'Easy Street.' When the money comes in from this, you and I are gonna blow this place and head for someplace that's warm all the time! Let's face it, Detroit isn't the nicest place to be in the winter."

Tracie sat up in bed. "Jimmy, I've heard you say things like this before, and I'm not doubting you, but why is this gonna be different than some of your other ideas?"

"This one is just foolproof. I've thought it out from every angle. It can't fail."

"And if it does, what's Jake gonna say about this?"

"Hey, Jake knows I'm good for the money. He wouldn't have loaned it to me if he didn't think he was gonna get it back."

"Honey, Jake has ways of getting his money back. He's not just a nice guy, you know."

"I know, but when this comes off, I'll pay him back with his lousy high interest, and still have plenty left over for us to split to Tahiti or someplace."

Tracie smiled. "Tahiti! God, that sounds nice."

Jimmy pulled Tracie towards him and kissed her. He loved the feel of her bare breasts pressing up against his chest. "It's gonna be great!"

"And you're sure the package with the bomb in it was switched with the package of diamonds?"

"I watched Heinrich make the switch myself. He sent the package to the airline as certified, and I walked out of the mine with the diamonds in my pocket. As soon as Flight 249 hits a higher altitude over the Atlantic that bomb goes off. When it is reported down, we collect the insurance money, and we still have the diamonds. Billy is gonna be coming home sometime soon, so we'll be able to take him with us when we leave."

Billy, Jimmy's son, was now eighteen and was the product of his first marriage. He was the world to Jimmy. He was on a trip to the Middle East before he started college.

"Don't you think your ex will have something to say about that?"

"He's old enough to decide for himself now. You think he's gonna choose this snow instead of warm sunshiny beaches?" Jimmy got out of bed. "Look, I've got to get back to the office. I want everything to appear as normal as possible until all of this is over."

Jimmy walked into the offices of Aberdeen Investments. As usual, Eileen, one of the company secretaries, was at the front desk. "Afternoon, Eileen. Any messages for me?"

"Just one. From Billy. He said the US State Department had ordered all US citizens out of Israel.

He ended up in Cairo and the state department had helped rearrange a bunch of flights so people could leave. He did manage to get a flight out to Detroit. He'll be in early tomorrow morning on Flight 249."

108

Wrath

Wrathful sinners being dismembered in Hell.

eaten by Anger

by Frank Zafiro

In the darkness of his cell, Phillipe Richard crouched on his haunches and put his back against the wall. The block guard called lights out an hour ago, but Richard couldn't sleep. He hardly ever could.

In prison, most men couldn't sleep out of fear.

For Richard, it was a simmering anger that kept him up. Just as soon as he'd start to fade into sleep, images popped in his mind. Almost always, it was that little punk Stefan Kopriva. *Le fils de pute!* Richard saw him over and over, how he tricked a confession from him outside the locker room. Then testifying against him in court. Playing his little tape recording. So smug.

Richard knew he would see Kopriva again.

He wouldn't be in here much longer.

The lawyer was good and the judge sympathetic, but most of it was simply because he was Phillipe Richard, hockey player. Grand-nephew of Maurice Richard, the Rocket, but he played like Dave "The Hammer" Shultz. On his way to the NHL on the power of his fists before that little piece of *merde—*

Richard stood, drew a long, deep breath and let it out.

He'd accepted a plea bargain. Three year sentence for manslaughter instead of second degree murder. He had twenty-two months left, counting good behavior.

His cell-mate slept peacefully on the top bunk. Richard stared at him malevolently, jealous of his repose. Todd's quiet breath filled the cell. The dainty outline of his chin, nose and mouth made Richard grind his teeth. They reminded him of Kopriva.

Mon Dieu, he should not have to stare at that.

He reached out and nudged Todd. The smaller man could roll over and face the wall. If Richard could not sleep, at least he didn't have to be reminded of Kopriva constantly.

Todd stirred awake and saw the hulking Richard looming over him. His eyes widened in panic.

"No, please! I—"

"Roll over."

"Don't hurt me," Todd whimpered. "I'll…I'll do what you want."

Richard's lip curled in disgust. "Relax. I am no *pédé.* I just want you to—"

"Please," he pleaded.

Richard clenched his jaw. He was Phillipe Richard, hockey player. Enforcer. He wasn't some kind of pervert. He loved women only, not—

"Just don't hurt me," Todd said.

Anger flared up in Richard. He reached out and grabbed Todd by the shoulder and jerked him upright.

Todd screamed.

Richard whipped a huge fist into Todd's face. He felt the cheekbone snap beneath his knuckles.

Todd screeched and thrashed on the bunk. Animal rage flooded Richard and he pumped his fist into Todd's head like a trip-hammer. He felt like he was on the ice again, gloves and sticks discarded, in the heat of battle. Kopriva's face flashed before him and he unleashed his hatred into each blow.

Light flooded the block. Richard punched.

Buzzers. Clanging metal. Cries of men.

His fists were wet. And red.

A jolt went through him and his body went rigid. He collapsed to the ground to the clacking, zapping sound of electric current. He couldn't move.

The current released him. A mass of bodies descended on him, pinning him to the ground. Someone ratcheted handcuffs onto his wrists.

"Oh, Jesus," someone else muttered.

One of the guards stood him up. Zimmerman. His eyes were round with wonder.

"Why'd you do it?" he asked Richard.

Richard glanced at the still form on the top bunk.

"Jesus, Richard," Zimmerman said. "You were out of here in twenty-three months."

"Twenty-two," Richard murmured, staring at Todd's collapsed face.

"Well, you'll do life now."

Phillipe Richard didn't answer.

artmann's Case

by John M. Floyd

Fran Valentine arrived at the sheriff's--her daughter Lucy's--office to find a sour-faced stranger standing there. Deputy Ed Malone nodded to her from a corner.

Fran eyed the new man. "Who're you?"

"FBI."

"Somebody blew up a mailbox, Mother," Lucy said, "and Agent Hartmann here heard about it. He's seen cases where credit card bills were stolen, and boxes destroyed as a coverup."

"Whose mailbox?" Fran asked.

"Joseph Dewberry's," Hartmann said.

"Impossible. Joey picks up his mail in town."

"Then what was mounted on the post beside his driveway?"

"A newspaper dropbox. And Joey has no credit cards."

Hartmann scowled. "You sure?"

"Trust me, she knows everything about this town," Lucy said.

"She know Dewberry's not home?" Hartmann asked.

"He's visiting, in Alabama," Fran said.

"I see. Ms... Valentine?"

"Fran."

"Well, Fran, mail destruction's a federal offense–"

"It's a newspaper box!"

"So you say. But I found a hole punched through the back of the wreckage. Probably for a fuse, or wiring." Hartmann lit a cigarette and tossed the pack and lighter onto the desktop beside Fran's purse. They almost knocked over the NO SMOKING sign.

Lucy said, "A neighbor saw a car leave several minutes before the blast, Mother–"

"They set a timer," Hartmann said. "Professionals."

Fran rolled her eyes. "Tomorrow's July fourth--this was probably a drunk hooligan with fireworks."

"Fireworks?"

She took several red balls from her purse. "Cherry bombs. For my nephew."

"Those fuses are too short. And amateurs don't set timed charges." Hartmann sneered. "Besides, it's my case now."

"Later, Mother," Lucy said.

"But, Luce, I think I know–"

"Later."

Fran scooped her purse off the desk. "Restroom break."

After Fran left Hartmann said, "Luce?"

"A nickname."

"How cute. Luce, Joey, Fran–" Hartmann smirked at Ed. "What do they call you? Eddie?"

"You can call me Deputy Malone."

"Everybody calm down," the sheriff said. For a long time no one spoke. Finally: "Mother's probably right. Pranksters."

Hartmann snorted. "Homemade fuses don't work. If you were smart you'd know that. That hole–"

Fran stomped back into the office. "How long was I gone?"

"Excuse me?"

"How long, just now?"

"I don't know--three minutes? Why?"

Suddenly an explosion rattled the windows.
Everyone jumped.

All except Fran. She was staring calmly at Agent
Hartmann.

"What'd you do?" he shouted.

"A little demo." From her purse Fran took out
Hartmann's pack and lighter. He gaped at the
desktop where they'd been. Fran shook out a
cigarette. "Old trick. Cut here, an inch from the end,
light up, tuck a cherry bomb's fuse into the cut, and
leave."

"But–what about the hole punched in the back of the
box?"

"Ventilation. Air flow keeps the butt burning.
Several minutes per inch of cigarette." She smiled.
"Rednecks aren't 'professionals,' Hartmann. They
just improvise."

He glared at her, hesitated, then marched to the door.
"Keep your damn case," he growled.

"Nice seeing you too," Lucy said.

"Don't worry, Luce," Fran said, as Hartmann's car
roared away. "All I blew up was a restroom
wastebasket."

Lucy frowned. "Hope Mabel wasn't back there, in a
stall." Mabel Pope had been helping with the filing.

"Might've done her good. I think she's been constipated, lately."

Ed Malone asked, "So who you figure did Joey's box? Billy Crowder?"

"Probably. Even sober, he hates the Dewberrys." Fran paused. "What're you two staring at?"

"How'd you know all that?" Lucy said. "The fuse stuff."

"An old friend. He was good at those things."

"What was he, an engineer?"

"A hooligan," Fran said. And grinned.

The Demon of Tobacco

Hear Her Roar

by Kimberly Brown

Queen Nore grasped the arms of the chair until her fingers felt bloodless, but it was her only show of tension. Her face remained calm, alert, as a good captain's should, though her stomach clenched as if a fist squeezed her insides. She ignored the dozen technicians who went about their business, adjusting the computers that kept the *Starship Athena* going.

Outside the starboard viewport of the ship, Nore's second-in-command, Rai, floated, hooked only by the umbilical of a fragile-looking tether. The skin of the huge starship had received damage from an asteroid shower they passed through, and Rai was the most experienced at repairing the tough outer TeLon covering.

Beside Nore stood Ara, a female lieutenant. She, too, watched Rai breathlessly, but her fear played across her face.

"Lieutenant." Nore said, "Have you nothing to do?"

Ara bowed her head and went to her station, but her eyes stayed on Rai.

Leaving the ship was a routine job, but no less dangerous for the amount of experience Rai had.

Nore's heart beat harder as she watched him work. His body was covered by the thin protective clothing and his handsome face was covered by the oxygen device.

Nore knew every crevice of that face--the silky dark skin, the intelligent green-brown eyes, the noble nose. In spite of the fact that she was ruler of their country back on earth, and Rai's superior on the ship, several months earlier she'd taken him into the captain's quarters, into her bed.

She'd loved the game they played, pretending an almost adversarial relationship by day, only to fall into each other's arms at night. When she watched his nimble fingers dance across the ship's controls like a pianist across the keys, when they passed in one of the narrow hallways, their bodies touching ever-so slightly, her heart fluttered like a giddy schoolgirl's.

Outside, Rai let go of a tool, storing it for a moment in the gravity-less space, as if on an invisible shelf. Then he reached to grab it, pulling the tether that bound him to the ship taut. Nore heard Ara gasp and mutter, "Be careful!"

He should be more careful, Nore agreed to herself. He should've been more careful last night, when the security cameras caught him sneaking into Ara's quarters.

He'd tried to skirt the cameras, and might have defeated them, except he didn't know about the hidden ones--the ones she'd placed in each room. A queen had to know what her subjects did, didn't she? Had to know the good as well as the bad? Well, she knew what Ara and Rai did last night and the knowledge made her stomach a pit of angry snakes.

She rose from her chair and moved to the control console, where she entered rapid commands. A couple of the technicians stared at her, but no one made a move to stop her.

More commands. Then, as the crew watched in horror, the tether came loose from the ship and Rai floated like the tool had floated only moments ago. But there was no one to grab him and bring him to safety. She could see his body react, twist, try to swim toward the ship. She could picture in her mind the horror on that handsome face. But it was too late. The ship was slowly moving away from him.

Then Nore turned on Ara, the anger in her stomach flaring once more. She lifted an arm. "Arrest this woman for treason against the Queen."

As security guards grabbed Ara, the snakes in Nore's stomach finally calmed.

a Llorona

by Sunny Frazier

Keening, high pitched, the sound grew in intensity.

"What was that? A wounded animal?"

Larry and nature were not a good match. Still, the cabin was my husband's idea. Isolation had its attractions.

"That's La Llorona. The Weeping Woman."

He looked around in the dense vegetation, peering into the darkness. "Where is she?"

"Dead." I continued to walk toward the river. The sound of water spilling over rocks engulfed me. It was like my white noise machine. Soothing. Unobtrusive.

"What I just heard didn't sound like a ghost."

"You heard the wailing. Hispanic folklore says she drowned her sons in the river and now she cries with torment."

"Ah, so this is another one of your grandmother's stories." Always the skeptic. Outwardly, he put on the face of political correctness at his legal practice Fresno. Privately, he was condescending of my

123

Hispanic heritage. The wedding was nearly called off when his blue-blooded parents found out my mother was Mexican.

"Okay, I'll bite," he scoffed. "Why did she kill her children?"

"For revenge." I turned and faced him. "It's an old story, supposedly true. An Indian girl named Maria caught the eye of a conquistador. He saw her dancing in a beautiful white dress and had to have her. Theirs was the first inter-racial marriage, her children the first *Mestizos*."

"But the husband had a wandering eye. One day, he was driving his Spanish mistress around in a beautiful carriage. He saw his family walking on a footpath by the river. Stopping, he spoke only to his sons, ignoring Maria. Enraged, she threw her children in the water to get even with the bastard."

A flicker of guilt crossed my husband's face. I knew about Tanya. Seething filled my soul. I watched him fidget.

"When she realized what she had done, she tried to pull her sons from the rapids. But it was too late."

"It seems like an extreme over-reaction on her part," Larry said uncomfortably.

"It was." I continued to saunter along the riverbank. "After the bodies were found and the boys were buried, she put on her favorite white gown. The people in her village watched her roam the riverbank, a doomed mother mourning for her dead children.

She became thinner, her beautiful dress dirty and tattered. Finally, she took poison and died. To this day her specter follows the currents, eternally searching for the lost souls of her children."

The keening again cut through the night. If La Llorona were an Irish myth, it would be the cry of the banshee. Every culture has women to fear.

"This is too weird. Let's go back to the cabin," my husband begged. Was pragmatic Larry suddenly nervous of the paranormal?

Opening his arms, he stepped toward me for a comforting hug. I had nothing to offer but disgust. I pushed him roughly away. The force was enough to send him toppling down the embankment.

"She's seeks revenge on adulterous husbands as well," I screamed, finally unleashing my own rage and hurt.

I heard the ear-piercing cry, so haunted and tortured. As I ran down the footpath to the cabin, her wails trailed my wake like a siren. Over my shoulder, I saw La Llorona, a wraith in white. Her skeletal fingers snaked around the neck of my cheating husband. Her triumphant cries drowned out his screams.

I blocked out the sound of frantic splashing with the words of my wise *abuelita*: "You must not say La Llorona's name aloud or go out after dark, *meja*. And never, never get caught between the Weeping Woman and the river."

Shot of Anger

by BJ Bourg

"You can't tell him—he'll kill you!"

Gina Baxter nodded. "Probably."

Richard Constant paced the floor. "Think about what you're saying. You can't—"

"My mind's made up." Gina walked to the door of the musky hotel room and paused. "Don't worry; I won't mention your name."

Gina drove home and glanced at her watch. Six o'clock. Heath was due back from work any minute. She removed his 12-gauge shotgun from the gun cabinet and stuffed it under the mattress in their bedroom. She had just smoothened out the quilt when she heard the hum of Heath's Ford Mustang pulling into the driveway. A minute later the front door opened.

"Baby, I'm home," Heath called from the kitchen. He slammed the door shut and his boots echoed across the kitchen floor. "Where's supper?"

Gina looked up from the sofa.

Heath stopped and cocked his head sideways. "What are you doing?"

"Waiting for you."

"Why didn't you cook?"

"I was busy."

"Busy? Doing what?"

Gina braced herself for what would happen next. "Having sex."

Heath's eyes widened. "Excuse me?"

"I was out at a hotel room, having sex."

"You were *what?*"

Gina swallowed hard. Her heart thumped in her chest. "I'm having an affair. I want out of this marriage."

Heath fell back against the doorframe and slid to the floor. He stared down at his hands and his pale face slowly turned to crimson. When he looked up, Gina felt a chill reverberate up and down her spine.

"Who with?"

Gina shook her head. "That's not important."

Heath pulled himself to his feet and flexed his hands. "I asked you a question. Who with?"

"I won't say."

Gina gasped as Heath closed the distance between
them and grabbed her around the throat. In one
motion, he jerked her to her feet and smashed her
back against the wall. He leaned close and Gina
smelled the stench of anger on his breath. "Who
with?"

Gina clutched at his hand. "Stop! I can't breath."

Heath squeezed tighter. "This one's going to hurt
really bad." He leaned back and punched Gina full in
the face. When he released his grip on her throat, she
crumbled to the floor. He stomped and kicked her
and then grabbed a handful of her hair.

As he'd often done when he was angry, he dragged
her into their bedroom and shoved her onto the bed.
He began removing his clothes. Ribs burning and
struggling to suck air into her lungs, Gina rolled off
the bed and grabbed the shotgun. She pointed it at
Heath's chest. "This is the last time!"

Heath looked up and his eyes widened. "What—?"

Gina pulled the trigger. The hollow, metallic click
was the loudest sound she'd ever heard.

Hell fire flickered in Heath's eyes. He snatched the
shotgun from Gina's grasp and racked a round into
the chamber. "You *bitch!*"

Gina squeezed her eyes shut just as Heath pulled the
trigger. The explosion was deafening. Gina's

nostrils burned. There was a loud thump and then all was quiet.

Gina slowly opened her eyes and stared through the smoke at Heath's lifeless body. The front of his face was a mass of broken flesh, blood, and protruding metal. The shotgun was beside his body, twisted and split. Despite the pain she felt, Gina smiled. There was no law against shoving wads of bubble gum down the barrel of your husband's shotgun. This would be written off as an accidental death and she would be viewed as the battered wife who cheated death.

Gina sighed. "Now, what to do with Richard's wife?"

Deer for a Deer

by Gary Hoffman

The blacktop road leading to the gravel road where Gustoff Helming lived was usually deserted, day or night. But that was fine with Gustoff. He preferred living in a rural area with few neighbors and no city noise. Gustoff was president of the school board and was on his way home from its monthly meeting in the small town of Elwood, the only town close to where he lived. It was a crisp November night, and Gustoff was enjoying the solitary ride.

He'd only gone a hundred yards on his gravel road when a large white-tailed deer jumped from the fence row and froze when Gustoff's headlights flashed into its eyes. Gustoff immediately saw the large rack on the deer. He stopped and slipped out the driver's door, taking his 30-06 rifle off the rack behind the seat. He steadied the rifle on the top of the door and fired once. The deer fell.

He put the rifle back and pulled his pickup to the side of the road. He took his flashlight and hunting knife with him as he approached the deer. He poked it to make sure it was dead. He then grabbed its antlers and dragged it a few feet away from the road. After he finished field dressing it, he wrangled it into the bed of his pickup and headed home.

Gustoff knew it wasn't deer season yet, but, hell, everyone in Gasconade County poached a deer once in a while. When he got home, he backed the pickup into his barn. He used a block and tackle hanging from a beam there and hoisted the deer. The carcass would cool tonight, and he would cut it up tomorrow.

He pulled the pickup from the barn and to the front of his house just as a car was coming up his driveway. His heart started to pound faster, and even on this chilly night, he started to sweat when he recognized the Game Warden emblem on the SUV. The new game warden for the county stepped out of the SUV. "Evenin', Gustoff."

"Fine night isn't it, Jim?"

"Well, I hope so, Gus. Got a report of someone poaching deer out this way. Know anything about that?"

"No, can't say that I do. Just got back from a meetin' in town myself."

Jim looked in the bed of Gustoff's truck with his flashlight. There was still a lot of blood there. "Care if I take a look in your barn?"

Gustoff was taken to the county sheriff's office where he had to post bond. He called everyone connected with county law enforcement every curse word he could think of. He kept insisting it was no big deal since everyone in the county poached sometime. He ranted enough about being arrested that most everyone in town knew about it the next morning.

Three nights later, Gustoff and his wife were coming back from buying groceries in town. As Gustoff drove over a small rise, a pickup was parked there. He was past it before he even got a good look at it. Then, in the field, he saw someone with a flashlight. He was still irate about being arrested. Yeah, they get me and let everyone else get away! Well, by God, if I can't do it, no one else can. He called the game poaching hotline as soon as he got home.

His phone rang an hour later. "Dad, this is Jerod. I was headed to your house tonight and got picked up for shooting a deer. I need some bond money."

# Sweet Revenge

by Deborah Elliott-Upton

One thing that drove Vickie bonkers was her sister-in-law always getting her way. Bethany proclaimed monthly family dinners mandatory. Being the eldest, she made the rules.

Bethany didn't like Vickie from their initial meeting and convinced the rest of the family they didn't care for her either. Vickie did the unspeakable: marrying their baby brother, Joey, without their permission.

Vickie's friend, Jean, suggested trying the old adage of catching more flies with honey. So, Vickie ran errands for Bethany, babysat her children and walked her dog. Bethany accepted the favors, but her feelings remained unchanged. Still, Vickie wanted Joey's family to love her since she had none of her own.

For the next family dinner, Bethany decreed Vickie bring dessert. Vickie chopped pecans, shredded fresh coconut and baked a luscious Italian Cream cake. When placing the crystal cake stand on Bethany's dining table near her father-in-law's seat of honor, Vickie was overjoyed. *How could they not love her creation?*

At dinner, her cake had been moved and in its place sat a pie. The family oohed and ahhed over the pie's aroma. Vickie tried not to show disappointment, but inside her heart hardened toward her sister-in-law. Why did she make a pie when I was bringing dessert? she wondered.

By the end of the evening, no one had touched Vickie's cake, except herself. She had sliced into it, leaving a perfect magazine photo-op. Inside, the cake looked more delectable than out – and the outside was bakery-perfect. Yet, the family ignored it and devoured Bethany's pie.

When she casually mentioned no one tried her dessert, Bethany said, "Daddy doesn't care for Italian Cream cake."

The next month, Vickie decided to fight fire with fire. She baked an overfilled and practically bursting from its flaky crust cherry pie. Bethany positioned an Italian Cream cake next to Daddy Leonard. "My favorite!" he exclaimed.

Vickie didn't eat dessert that night, so her pie traveled back home exactly as it came.

"You'd have thought I brought a poison pie," Vickie later told Jean. "Why'd she lie? Why do they hate me?" Anger welled up inside her like a tsunami with nowhere to go.

"Wish I could eat your pies," said Jean, the diabetic. "You can always kill them with kindness."

"That's a good idea."

"It smells wonderful in here," Joey said.

"It's the Italian Cream cake I'm taking to the family dinner. You know it's your daddy's favorite." She handed Joey the spoon, frosting still clinging to it and glistening with pecans and coconut. "Bethany's making a pie for tonight." Her lips tightened. "Eat pie and die."

As she carefully placed the crystal cake cover over the cake, he laughed, but Vickie didn't.

Just before dinner, Vickie slipped into the dining room. She leaned over to inhale the fresh floral arrangement. Parked in front of Daddy Leonard's water glass set a pie, crusted with almonds. She reached into her pocket and withdrew a needle she'd borrowed from Jean. One quick injection in the pie's middle between the almonds disappeared when she removed the needle. Cherry juice bubbled up, erasing the insertion.

As expected, the in-laws passed over her cake in favor of Bethany's pie. While she ate the lone slice of cake, Vickie watched her husband gobble the pie like the rest of his family. He'd been warned, she thought. But his family always did whatever Bethany wanted. She made the rules.

Envy

The envious being submersed in freezing
water in Hell.

ish

by Frank Zafiro

I wish I were Chinese.

I watched the young man through the rifle scope. My crosshairs bobbed from his chin to his forehead.

To be that small and compact. To move with that grace. Like Bruce Lee instead of a lanky, gangly nobody. That'd be much better.

The Chinese man stopped walking and sat down on the bench, draped his arms over the back and basked in the sun. Completely oblivious of his great fortune in being Asian. Unaware of me. I touched the trigger ever so slightly, but decided to wait. The heavy door at the clock tower base was locked. My boss had the only other key, but if I started shooting, I knew the cops would reach me quickly. The time wasn't right.

I shifted the scope and scanned the pathway. Two pudgy secretaries in office clothing and tennis shoes hurry-walked past the Chinese man. I wasn't fat like them, but I wished I had enough money for a gym membership. Some muscle on this frame would make a difference.

I pulled away and rubbed my eye. The backpack lay on the floor next to me. It was barely large enough to conceal the rifle when broken down. There wasn't any room left over for a lunch, which was where my boss thought I was. Eating lunch somewhere. Not at the top of the clock tower, looking down.

With a smile, I put my eye back to the scope. Both it and the rifle cost more than I made in a month, but it was worth it.

Further along the path, a trim brunette sat at another bench. She read a paperback intently and ignored all passersby. The swell of her breasts inside the tight yellow blouse she wore created some wonderful cleavage. I focused on that image and wished for the thousandth time that I had a steady woman. I was tired of paying for it or settling for the ones that looked like the pudgy secretaries.

I adjusted the zoom and stared at her lovely chest and bare legs just below the hem of her short skirt. After a while, I don't know how long, a rush of blue crossed my field of fire. I zoomed back.

A businessman walked by, ogling the brunette. She didn't notice. He slowed, leered and moved on. I wished I had the money to look like that. I'd talk to that girl, book or no book. I'd date her and sleep with her and I wouldn't have to pay her, either. What was he doing looking at her like that, anyway? I wish—

"*Rodney?*" squawked my walkie-talkie.

I muttered a curse and moved my hand from the gun stock to push the button. "Yeah, boss?"

"Where the hell are you?" Darryl asked.

I swept the scope far to the left and found the maintenance shed. Darryl stood by the open door, one hand on his hip. The other held his walkie-talkie.

"Lunch," I answered.

"Lunch is over. Meet me at the maintenance shed. Whoever is running their dogs at night left a half dozen piles for you to clean up near the slides."

I set the walkie-talkie on the ledge next to me and put the cross-hair between Darryl's eyes. I wished I were the fucking boss. I wished he was the one that had to go scoop the dog shit.

"Rodney? You hear me?"

I tickled the trigger.

"Rodney, Goddamnit!"

I sighed and reached for the walkie-talkie. "On my way."

"Now!"

Reluctantly, I unsnapped the scope and disassembled the rifle.

I wish I weren't a coward.

reen-eyed monster

by Kimberly Brown

Gerta Goldman lit the cook stove and stood for a moment, enjoying its warmth. From the farmhouse window, she could see her sons, Max and Josef, walking through the gate. Across the cobblestone street, she saw the small dark child, hanging on his own gate, watching as he always did when her sons came home.

"Max," Gerta called to her oldest through the open window. "Invite the boy to play." She dried her hands on her apron and brushed dust out of her long skirt.

Max grumbled, but went to do her bidding. Josef, still a baby at four, ran through the door and jumped into her arms.

"Why do we have to play with him, Mama?"

"Because he's lonely. And his father died not long ago," Gerta said. "Think of how you'd feel if your papa died."

Max led the boy into the house, where he studied the room with his big eyes. Gerta had visited his home, to take a pudding to the wake of his father, and had been distressed at how stark the place was. The family was not poor--the boy's father had been a government official and, while not wealthy, had done well enough. But the house hadn't felt like a home, at least not to Gerta, who loved her home noisy with her sons' squealing laughter.

He was not an ugly boy, though small for his seven years, and pale of face. He was polite enough, but unkempt. Gerta couldn't help but think the boy must be confused-- his father had beat him regularly and his mother Klara treated him like an infant, as if to make up for it. He watched Gerta and her family with such a hunger to be included. He must long for a normal life, Gerta had often thought. He had to be troubled by his father's death, surely. But the old man's death had to have caused, if not happiness, then relief. Gerta shook her head at the thought of such a father.

As the boys played, Gerta began to prepare their Sabbath feast. When she next glanced out the kitchen window, she saw Aaron returning home, the *challah* loaves for their dinner under his arm. Josef and Max ran through the house to greet him, Josef throwing himself into Aaron's arms with joy.

"Liebchen," she said to the dark, watchful child. She knelt in front of him and took his grimy hands in hers. "You should go home now." She remembered one of the most severe beatings had happened when she had given the boy a bite of the *challah*. She had heard the obscenities the father screamed. The father was dead now, but his rules were still his rules.

Aaron came in and hung his coat. He looked at the boy sternly. Gerta knew Aaron also remembered the beating, the father screaming "dirty Jews" as he hit the boy. It had been all Gerta could do to hold him back, prevent him from rushing across the road in defense of the boy. "It's not our business," she had said, but she and Aaron had both trembled with anger.

"Adolf," Aaron said. "You must go home now. Our Sabbath is not for you."

With a hungry, jealous look cast over his thin shoulder, the boy went back to his lifeless home.

ustom Design

by John M. Floyd

The two brothers lived together in the city at the end of the valley at the foot of the great blue mountains. In fact they did almost everything together, including a recent stretch in prison. Nothing unusual, in these parts. Compared to the rest of the town, they were model citizens.

On this particular morning, as they were about to eat breakfast in their ramshackle house, one of them made a sobering discovery.

"There ain't nothin' to eat," he said, looking annoyed.

His younger and shorter brother, who was unfortunately his equal in the brains department, gave that some thought. "We could ask the neighbor for a handout," he said.

"Good idea. But why ask? Let's just go take what we want."

Shorty shook his head. "He's got a couple mean dogs." He rose and went to the window, where he peered out at their neighbor's house. "Wish we had one of his pigs. I saw two fat ones running around over there yesterday..."

Suddenly his eyes widened.

The taller of the brothers hurried to the window. When he looked out also, his mouth dropped open.

Together they pushed through the door and sprinted across the street. Their neighbor, a thin fellow who rarely smiled, stood beside his driveway with his hands in his pockets, studying the object that had just caused the two brothers such surprise.

"Where'd that come from?" the taller one blurted.

The solemn-faced man turned and regarded them a moment. "From behind my house. I just finished it."

"Wow," Shorty said, staring. "Wish we had one of these."

"Will it work?" his brother asked.

The man scowled at him. "Of course it'll work. And don't touch it, please."

Shorty withdrew an outstretched hand. The brothers exchanged a look. "We could try it out for you."

"I think I can manage."

"When?"

"Soon."

A silence passed. Clearly fascinated, Shorty asked, "How about taking us along, at least?"

146

"Can't," the neighbor said. "This is business, not pleasure."

The brothers looked stricken. "But why not?" the taller one asked. Then he seemed to remember something. "Our cousin'd look after all your pets while we're gone."

"Afraid not." The man frowned. "By the way, one of my two chickens is missing. You boys know anything about that?"

Both of them shook their heads so hard their jaws flapped.

"And my son says his new wagon's gone."

More headshaking.

"Well, see that you leave my animals alone, from now on."

Another look passed between the brothers. Shorty said, pointing at the strange contraption, "Look, we asked you real nice. We could be a big help, on this."

"Sorry." The man scratched his beard. "Besides, it's not mine. It was built under contract."

"What's that mean? You got to deliver it?"

"In a way. Now, if you'll excuse me..."

The brothers watched him turn away. "You're making a mistake," Shorty said, with a touch of menace in his voice.

147

The thin man stopped. "Pardon?"

"Take us along," the tall brother said, his face darkening, "or you'll be sorry."

"And why is that?"

Shorty glanced around for their neighbor's dogs. Seeing neither of them, he pulled a long, ugly knife from inside his belt and held it up. "Because, if you don't," he said, "we'll be waiting for you when you get back."

At that moment, thunder grumbled in the mountains above the town. Noah turned and looked in that direction, then faced the two men again. His eyes were sad and thoughtful.

"I doubt it," he said.

he Perfect Husband

By Deborah Elliott-Upton

"Your life's perfect! Perfect job, house *and* body," Megan said. "What more could a woman want?"

"Your perfect husband," Caroline answered, sipping the Chardonnay.

"No such animal."

"I'll take him *and* a baby."

"Richard's not father material." Megan sighed. "No one's gonna take my man."

***

Home from a business trip seven months later, Caroline sat across from Richard, her new husband, at the same restaurant. Tonight she'd tell him she was pregnant.

"A whirlwind romance," their friends said, nodding. "Comforting each other after Megan's sudden death drew them closer."

When the salads arrived, Richard paled. "We said NO mushrooms."

Caroline's hand covered his. "Darling, *I* can't have shellfish. *You* can't have peanuts." She stared into his eyes, feeling like Svengali. "Megan would want us to be happy."

Richard's response was to return to the bar and in haste, dropped his knife. Caroline started to retrieve the silver, then thought better. *People are paid for that.*

The knife was not the only thing left behind unnoticed. Caroline hated Richard's thoughtlessness. Like Hansel and Gretel's breadcrumbs, his clothing spread a trail behind him. His toothpaste's perpetual missing cap, yard tools left outside to rust from infrequent use and newspapers strewn everywhere were routine. He'd forget to call if he ran late or met friends after work for drinks.

When Richard returned, his eyes strayed to an athletic-looking blonde. Caroline touched her flawless abs. Soon she'd have a round belly. Before Megan's death, he's joked about her weight problems. Caroline remembered Megan drank heavily after such remarks from *their* husband.

Richard fell short of perfect in many respects. He didn't mind her being the chief breadwinner and lately, his commissions took a dive. Unfortunately, his buying habits never declined. Talking about budgets always put him in a bad mood, as did subjects involving responsibility.

How would Richard take news of fatherhood? With each passing year, Caroline's hopes of becoming a mother decreased. For her, this *was* the right time.

Megan said he wasn't father material. Caroline's brain searched for tidbits of their conversations.

"He forgets to put away poisonous cleansers when my niece visits …left out the pruning shears while the neighbor's kids played outside …knows I'm allergic to mushrooms, yet didn't mention Katie's meatloaf contained them …I could've died."

And she had died from ground mushrooms added to a church potluck casserole. The autopsy revealed an allergic reaction, but no one remembered Megan eating mushrooms. None would ever suspect her best friend, Caroline. Envy of Megan's perfect husband led Caroline to do the unspeakable. Now, with full clarity, she remembered Megan's words, "No one's gonna take my man." Caroline realized the sigh wasn't one of determination, but of desperation.

No one's gonna take my baby, Caroline thought. If they divorced, he'd ask for shared custody and demand alimony. In this state, he'd likely get both.

When Richard excused himself again, Caroline noticed he blatantly ogled the blonde and winked before staggering toward the bar.

Definitely not father material.

The waiter came for their dessert order and Caroline knew the meal's perfect finishing touch. Richard never turned down chocolate cake. Thinking of the baby, she ordered a fruit medley for herself. She retrieved his fallen knife and opened her purse holding the airline's packaged peanuts she'd saved. Carefully, she mashed the nuts into a creamy paste.

151

When his cake arrived, she mixed the nuts into the frosting.

Back at the table, Richard shoved the chocolate into his mouth like it was his last meal.

Megan was wrong. Richard *was* the perfect husband. One with great insurance.

niper's Choice

By BJ Bourg

I took a deep breath and exhaled. "Okay, I'm ready."

The instructor began the countdown. When he said, "Fire," I dropped to the ground and pulled the butt of the sniper rifle snug into my shoulder. When the crosshairs locked on the lemon at one hundred yards, I squeezed off the shot. It exploded. My body went into autopilot. I bolted a fresh round and took out the next target. My hand was like a machine. I fired until my rifle was empty and my targets were only a misty memory.

"Eighteen seconds!" the instructor bellowed.

I smiled inwardly. Thus far, my overall time was the best. There was only one sniper left in the competition—my partner, and she wasn't even close to being in my league.

I stepped off the line and Skyler walked past me with her rifle. "That was awesome, Blake!"

I smiled and took my seat under the awning. As Skyler began shooting, I glanced over at the Top Gun Trophy. "That'll look good on my—"

"Thirteen seconds!"

My head jerked around. "That's impossible!"

Skyler's smile was wide. The other snipers crowded around and slapped her back. She pushed through them and jumped into my arms. I forced a smile. "Good job, Sky."

The instructor walked up and glanced down at his clipboard. "As of now, Skyler Conner's in first place and Blake Morgan's in second."

One of the snipers jabbed my shoulder. "Ha! You're losing to a girl!"

My chest burned.

The instructor looked at Skyler. "Do tomorrow what you did today, and you're taking that trophy home. Blake, you should be proud. This is the first time we've had two snipers from the same department competing for first place. You've trained her well."

***

Over supper, I didn't hear a word Skyler said. My mind was on the final competition. I couldn't lose to her. I'd trained her. The rest of the department would never let me live it down.

"You listening to me?"

I glanced up. "Yeah, sorry. Hey, let's walk down to the bar."

"You said we shouldn't drink while attending sniper school."

"It's okay. This one's in the bag."

We left the restaurant and walked down a narrow street to a dumpy, biker-looking bar. When we entered, Skyler took an uneasy look around. "You have your pistol?"

"Relax, we're cops." I ordered Skyler's favorite— Tequila shots. "To you!"

Skyler gulped down her shot. I lifted the glass to my mouth, but shielded it with my hand and placed it back on the bar untouched. As the night wore on, I fed Skyler shot after shot until she couldn't stand straight. When the bar closed, we left walking down the dark street. Skyler leaned against me and mumbled. The trophy was mine—no doubt. A pang of guilt tugged at my heart.

Footsteps approached quickly from behind and I turned. Something thumped against my temple. A bright light flashed inside my skull and my knees buckled. I fell hard.

A gruff voice hollered, "Give me your wallet!"

Through blurry vision, I saw Skyler fighting with a man. He knocked her to the ground. I struggled to my feet just as he turned. Skyler's pistol was in his hand and he immediately fired two shots into my chest. I collapsed. Each breath brought fire into my lungs. Footsteps retreated. My eyes dimmed. Someone shook me. I tried to focus—it was Skyler. Her face was streaked with tears.

"I'm so sorry!" she wailed.

I opened my mouth to explain, to release her of the guilt, but only blood poured out...

Demon embracing a woman

Foot In The Door

by Sunny Frazier

The idea of ripping off Brison Hart occurred to me while I was installing the security system to his renovated Tudor mansion in San Marino.

I knew Brison better than I wanted. We'd been frat brothers at business college, colleagues at Concepts, Inc., a corporate think tank for low-end ideas. He was my friendly competition in the early '70's. Now, I was reduced to setting up motion sensors for rich people like him.

Our investment choices were the fork in the road. That's where my life ended and Brison's began.

"These are the wave of the future," Brison announced one morning in the early '80's. He set a shoe box on my desk.

I opened the box and peered inside. "The future rests on a pair of sneakers?"

"These are beyond sneakers," he said, caressing the shoes. "In a few years, they will be on the foot of every man, woman and child. People will run in them, play in them, wear them to black-tie dinners."

Brison raved on about a man in Beverton, Oregon, who poured liquid rubber into his wife's waffle iron and produced the "waffle sole" of the sneaker. "The company is called 'Nike,' after the Greek goddess of Victory. Remember that name. The company just went public and stock is going fast." He invested $50,000 dollars on a hope and a Swoosh.

I had my own investment strategy.

The cold war was over, gas prices were high, and America was ready for the ultimate cost-efficient car. The prices on Japanese models were climbing. I topped Brison by putting $75,000, my entire life savings, into the automobile of the future. The time was ripe for the Yugo.

In the past, I'd had faith in eight-track decks, believed in the Beta Max, as well as the longevity of leisure suits. Now, I gambled that the little communist coupe was my ticket to a better lifestyle. What I didn't count on was the tenaciousness of Detroit and the patriotism of the American buyer.

Besides, the car sucked.

The company went bankrupt in 1989. NATO bombed the plant in Zastava, Yugoslavia. My wife divorced me, the bank foreclosed on my house, corporate downsizing left me jobless.

It wasn't fair that I should suffer because of a bad business decision while Brison prospered. It was time to take what I always felt should have been mine.

I cased the place while I worked on the installation of the alarm system. Brison was the perfect target. He had everything, including a day planner on the desk in the study.

I picked a night when he was scheduled to attend a social gala honoring whatever the filthy rich deem worth their honor. I knew the schematic of the system and how to disable it. In no time at all, I was in through the French doors leading from the pool area. That was the easy part.

Once inside, confusion set in. I hadn't put much thought into what I specifically wanted to steal. I just knew I wanted it all.

The titanium golf clubs in the closet were tempting. The 100-year-old bottle of Scotch at the bar would go down smoothly. My old college buddy was never into bling, but maybe there'd be a Rolex or two in the bedroom, a few diamond trinkets in his wife's jewelry box.

I entered the bedroom. A light clicked on and I found myself staring down the barrel of a gun. And not just any gun. In Brison's hand was a Desert Eagle .44 Magnum pistol.

I couldn't stop myself from coveting the gun that would kill me.

A Fable of Gardens

by Gary Hoffman

The competition for opulent houses had finally
calmed down in the Lake Maria subdivision.
Numbers of rooms, bathrooms, and all the bells and
whistles accompanying them were given up as a
draw. But, competitors being competitors, some sort
of contest seemed destined to continue. The
engagements moved from the houses onto the lawns
and yards. Massive, complicated gardens were now
being constructed.

Charles Hamilton felt he was losing the garden battle
until he came up with a brilliant idea. He constructed
a cave in his back yard and hired a hermit to live in it.
The "hermit" was actually a college student who ran
out of funds to attend classes. His job was to live in
the cave, not cut his hair or beard, and wave at
anyone who came into the gardens.

The idea took off like a spooked cat. The first
weekend, almost fifty people visited the Hamilton
Hermit. The following weekend it was over two
hundred, and by the third weekend, almost a
thousand. Charles then insisted on a contract with
the hermit to insure his new-found popularity.

The hermit wasn't overjoyed with his new solitary
life because it was boring compared to his college

days, but the contract offered a great deal of money. He signed using an alias in case he wanted out of the deal.

But, fame soon turned against Hamilton. People wanted nothing to do with Charles or his gardens. They were only interested in the hermit. Television crews came to film and interview the hermit, but never even spoke to Charles. These were the only high points in the hermit's life. Charles got to the point where he couldn't stand the man, but he knew the contract was iron-clad for both of them. He spoke with his wife about his problem, who thought the idea was rather ridiculous from the outset, but she had an idea.

Two days later, Felicia Hamilton had a crew of illegal migrant workers trimming shrubs in the back part of their property. She told the one who could speak some pidgin English what was going to happen, or she would turn them in to the authorities. A man was going to bring them cold drinks. They were to kill this man. Since they were trimming shrubbery, they would put the body through the shredder they were using.

She then went into the house and got four cold beers out of the fridge. She walked through their gardens. When she was right by the cave, her husband made a prearranged call to her on her cell phone. It rang loud enough for the hermit to hear it. She pretended to take the call and then looked into the cave at the hermit. "Hey, I need some help."

"What's that, ma'am?"

"I told those guys working out back I'd bring them a cold beer. My husband just called and said his car broke down. I need to go pick him up."

"Won't Mr. Hamilton get mad if I leave the cave?"

She winked at him. "He's not here, and I sure won't tell. Just take the beer and deliver it to them out the back gate."

"Ok." The hermit took the beer and started toward the end of the garden. Felicia went back to the house. The hermit looked around and saw her go out of sight, then snuck out a side gate instead.

Charles waited until he felt enough time had passed for the deed to be completed. He carried four more beers out to the men as an extra reward.

Pride

The prideful being broken on the wheel in Hell.

ride Goeth

by Frank Zafiro

The bell rang. I staggered to my corner. Reggie put the stool down and stepped through the ropes.

I sat down and B.J. went to work on my eye.

Reggie squeezed some water.

"How is it, Beege?"

I spit.

"Not good," B.J. answered. "Another round. If he dances."

Reggie grabbed my chin. "You hear that?"

I grunted. My chest burned. My whole body felt like melting rubber.

Reggie eyed me carefully. "Four down, six to go."

Wrong. One.

"You've gotta move, Paul," he said. "Stick and move."

I glanced over my shoulder into the crowd. Dominic Bracco sat in the front row. He met my eye with a hard stare. Still mad I turned down his offer, I guess.

"Down in the fourth," he'd said, and offered me five grand.

I said no can do. He swore this would be my last fight.

"You're a wash-up, anyway," he said.

Maybe he was right. Former regional champion until I lost to a kid last March. My stock fell, but I still had some regional name recognition. That got this fight with another up-and-comer. But all along, Bracco was behind the scenes, setting it up for a long odds payoff. Pick the round the old man goes down. Win a stuffed bear.

Reggie pulled my chin again. "Forget about that crooked sonofabitch," he said, pointing across the ring. "Worry about that sonofabitch over there!"

Long odds. Washed up old man. Didn't train this time around. Sucking wind. Roll of fat around the middle.

B.J. finished working on my eye. "Coupla shots, that'll open up again," he whispered.

"Circle away from his jab," Reggie said.

Long odds. Three-to-one against me. Nineteen-to-one against a win by knockout in the fifth. I put two thousand on that. Two thousand to make thirty-eight. I was good enough to pick the round.

The buzzer sounded. I rose wearily.

"Away from the jab," Reggie said on his way through the ropes and down the stairs.

Fifth round. I thought I was skilled enough to drop this kid at will.

Pride goeth before a fall, my mom used to say.

I don't think she ever meant it to be so literal.

The bell rang.

The kid came at me like a tank, snapping out his stiff jab. I slipped it and circled away.

The crowd yelled encouragement to him, eager for my blood.

I slipped another left, then absorbed a right hook to the body, turning away from the worst of it.

I circled.

The kid flicked his jab out toward my face. I twitched my head away, but the second caught me on the brow. He followed with a straight right. First, the thud and then I felt the trickle.

The sight of my blood got him excited and he waded in, throwing bombs. I took most of them off the arms. Then, just as he reared back for a left hook, I stepped in tight and blasted a right uppercut into his jaw.

The kid stutter-stepped backward two steps. His eyelids fluttered. I'd seen that before. He was out on his feet.

I looked into the crowd. I stared at Bracco. A surprised cheer went up. A moment later, the kid hit the canvas in a dead fall. Bracco stood and stalked out, his flunkies in tow.

I didn't bother to raise my arms in the air. I stumbled back to my corner. B.J. pressed a compress against my cut, grinning hugely.

Reggie shook his head in wonder.

Long odds.

Pride goeth before a fall.

Some sins you don't pay for. At least not right away.

Matter of Honor

by John M. Floyd

Morgan Hobbs lowered his newspaper. Twenty feet from his rocking chair on the hotel's porch, a young man was standing alone in the street.

"I'm callin' you out, mister."

Hobbs and the old man sitting beside him exchanged a glance.

"What's your name, son?" Hobbs said.

"I ain't your son. Name's Jim Parker."

"And?"

"I intend to kill you."

"But why?"

Parker raised his chin. "I'm told you insulted my wife."

"I don't even know your wife."

"Then you shouldn't've insulted her."

"Insulted her how?"

Parker cleared his throat. "Her... honor."

Hobbs removed a cigar from his pocket. "Who told you this?"

"Didn't give his name. He's at the saloon, got one ear missing."

Hobbs took a match from the old man and lit the cigar. "And you believe him?"

"You're denying you insulted her?"

"Yep."

"Why should I believe you over him? You're not from here."

"Neither's he, if you don't know his name." Puffing, Hobbs fanned out his match. "I'm here on business."

"What kind?"

"Looking for somebody. Woodrow Temple. Heard of him?"

"No."

"Killed a friend of mine. Shot him in the back."

"You the Law?"

"Temple'll wish I was, when I find him."

Parker snorted. "I don't care why you're here. We fighting or not?"

Hobbs squinted at him though a cloud of smoke, then turned again to the old man. "You gonna say anything?"

"Your affair, Dingo. Not mine."

Parker blinked. The words hung there in the dusty air. "You're Dingo Hobbs?"

"I prefer Morgan," Hobbs said.

But Parker's face had already changed. His gun hand drifted over to fiddle with his shirt buttons.

"If you're Dingo Hobbs, and I draw on you," he said, "you'll kill me deader'n a pine knot."

"No need for that. Go on home, let me finish reading the news."

The young man swallowed. Sweating. "It's not that simple."

Hobbs looked past him at the gathering crowd. "Now's not the time, son, to worry about pride."

A sad but determined look flickered in Jim Parker's eyes, and Hobbs realized this wasn't going to work.

"What's she look like, your wife?"

Parker frowned. "What?"

"You heard me. Tall? Short?"

"Short, and redheaded. What does that—"

"And she's not home right now, is she?"

"What? Course she's home."

"You sure?" Hobbs studied Parker's mud-caked pantslegs. "You come straight here from home?"

Parker hesitated. "I been settin' fenceposts. Why?"

"Well, when me and my friend here rode in awhile ago, a one-eared man was hugging a gal like you described, in yonder alley."

"What?!"

"Maybe someone wants you dead, Parker. Maybe he's lying, to get him both a lady and a ranch."

Parker seemed to consider that. And the more he considered the darker his face became.

"I'll excuse you," Hobbs said, "if you're needed elsewhere."

Parker nodded. "Much obliged. I believe I am."

Hobbs watched him march to the saloon. He paused outside the batwing doors, jaw set, then pushed inside.

"Hope you know what you're doin'," the old man said.

Hobbs snapped open his newspaper. "What do you mean?"

172

"I mean my eyes ain't bad, and I don't recall seeing no woman in an alley."

"Me neither," Hobbs said, around his cigar. "But Temple musta seen *us*. The fact he made up that story shows he's desperate."

"Like I said, hope you did right."

"What I did was save that kid's life. Or maybe my own."

"Yours?"

Hobbs shrugged. "He looked like he'd be fast."

"Faster'n you?"

"Don't know," Hobbs said, glancing at the saloon. "But I know one thing."

"What's that?"

Hobbs smiled. "He'll be faster'n Woodrow Temple."

ontgomery's Marvelous Machine

by Kimberly Brown

Professor Franklin Montgomery stood over Annabelle Ashburn's body and tried to stop trembling. It was all her fault. He flexed his fingers-- the same fingers that had clenched her slender throat just moments ago.

This slip of a girl had demanded half ownership in his time machine. *His* machine! Just because she'd helped with--what did she call it?-- the physics of the thing, she'd demanded that the machine be renamed "Ashburn-Montgomery's Marvelous Machine." That took away the pizzazz, the alliteration!

He wanted to hide her body and run, but he had to present the machine in just moments at the Great Exhibition of 1914, in his own home town, Danvers, Massachusetts. It was his day of glory.

Then an idea bloomed in his head. His presentation would proceed. He would go forward in time, except he wouldn't return. He would leave the machine behind, though, and it would bear his name and *only* his.

174

Someone rapped on the door. "Professor! Miss Ashburn! It's time."

"All right!" Montgomery put on his best cloak and top hat. He felt like a third-rate magician preparing to pull rabbits out of a hat. But he was a scientist.

Montgomery stepped into the hallway and shut the door. Through the velvet curtain, he heard the crowd buzz. The machine had been placed onstage, closely guarded by several well-paid street thugs.

Montgomery stepped onto the stage to wild applause. His chest swelled as he began his presentation. He didn't go into the physics that made the thing work, but he told himself, that was so the idea couldn't be stolen until it was securely patented. Deep down, he knew better. The knowledge had died with Annabelle. The machine would never be replicated, at least not by him.

"Now, ladies and gentlemen, I will go forward in time. I may stay months, even years. But I'll set my return to just moments from now, so practically no time will pass here."

The crowd gasped and he heard disbelieving laughter. "As proof, I'll bring back a dated newspaper," he said.

The crowd rumbled and he knew they wouldn't believe him, no matter what happened. A dated newspaper could be faked. But none of it mattered, because he'd never return.

Montgomery stepped into the wooden box. The crowd was quiet. Through the thin walls, Montgomery heard a scream from backstage. Someone had found Annabelle! His hands trembled as he twisted the knobs. Sweat trickled into his eyes. He couldn't remember which knob did what. The commotion from outside the box grew and he hit the big button, the one Annabelle had called the "go" button.

The box shook. Montgomery was thrown to the ground as the world whirled around him like a sickening carousel. Finally he landed with a thud, the wind knocked out of him. Eyes tightly closed, he heard only silence. Wherever he was, he was alive, and he wasn't in the Exhibit Hall!

Montgomery fought back nausea. When he was able to stand, his knees quaking, he found himself in a small, plain room. Three men sat at a table, their heads covered with white wigs, their mouths open in surprise. Standing in front of them was a dirty woman, her hands tied behind her back.

Montgomery heard a gasp behind him. A half-dozen young women stood, huddled together. One of them lifted her arm and pointed. "A true witch!"

Two husky young men strode forward and grasped Montgomery's arms. Panic rose in Montgomery's chest as he realized what had happened. He'd gone back, not forward. Back to when Danvers was called Salem Village.

Killer Brushstrokes

by Deborah Elliott-Upton

Amanda was the best artist in Dylan's class. She loved the way he fawned over her paintings. The instructor even hung several in simple frames in his gallery.

"The better the painting, the plainer the frame," Dylan explained. "Ornate frames means the art needs help to make a statement. Yours never does."

Amanda's heart swelled when Dylan said such things, but when he repeated them for the other students, it was nicer. With each compliment, Amanda felt like a glowworm with her cheeks on fire, which others said revealed her humility.

"When will you be back?" Amanda asked her teacher.

"There's a new artist, Marco, I heard about in London. A couple of weeks."

"New classes then?"

"Amanda, you don't *need* classes any more."

But she did. Although her art released her creativity, it wasn't enough. She needed public appreciation.

177

As much as the expression of her art, she needed Dylan's compliments.

Amanda hated Dylan's trips to secure paintings for the gallery, robbing time from art classes. When Dylan returned, Amanda was elated. Soon, she'd amaze fellow students with another masterpiece – one Dylan would place in the gallery for all to admire.

Dylan brought several of Marco's paintings. Although of no significance to Amanda, she pretended to approve of the purchases. Unfortunately, Dylan had another surprise.

"Sasha will learn much from such an accomplished artist as you," he said, introducing his protégé.

A protégé? Amanda always thought of herself as Dylan's protégé.

Dylan raved about your paintings," Sasha said.

As Dylan guided Sasha through the gallery, Amanda begrudgingly tagged along. He pointed out Amanda's work with the usual compliments. Sasha gushed accordingly over the paintings, so Amanda decided to give the girl a chance. Perhaps his protégé would be okay.

Sasha was a phenomenal student, picking up on brushstrokes almost as fast as Dylan demonstrated them. "Flair can't be taught. Sasha is a natural, like Grandma Moses," he said.

Amanda seethed inside while her art took second place to the new teacher's pet. Worse than listening to Dylan's accolades was Sasha's reactions. "I abhor limelight," she said, innocence surrounding her like a halo. "Amanda's been a gracious teacher, too. I owe any success to her."

Not that Amanda bought that for a moment. Hatred for Sasha rose like bile to her throat. She couldn't admit she'd been beaten. Pride held her captive until Dylan replaced one of Amanda's paintings with Sasha's in the gallery. I must protect my reputation, she thought. Sasha couldn't be allowed to steal that, too. She already had Dylan's affections. Amanda decided her rival deserved ornate frames. *Why can't Dylan see beyond her fake sweetness?*

After class, Amanda invited Sasha to join her in a walk. "This way," Amanda said. "The woods always inspire me."

Sasha followed like an eager puppy.

When they'd walked for several minutes, Amanda pointed to the right. "Look at the deer!"

Sasha squinted. "I don't see—"

With all her strength, Amanda swung the fallen limb across the back of Sasha's head.

The protégé crumpled to the soft soil, blood oozing from her cracked skull.

***

Amanda swished vivid splashes of crimson across the canvas,

Dylan studied the killer brushstrokes. "I can't imagine why Sasha suddenly disappeared. I'm so worried."

"Don't be." Amanda shrugged and stepped back from the easel. "She's probably somewhere exotic painting alongside the next Michelangelo. You've heard her speak of Marco, of course."

"I didn't realize–"

"Sasha's a natural artist. Probably gone Bohemian." Amanda smiled. "So, what do you think?" she asked, knowing once again, she was the best artist in Dylan's class.

he Bully of Backswitch

by Gary Hoffman

Billy Jo Collins had been drinking for a couple of
hours before Zeb Sellers walked into Mooney's
Loco-Weed Tavern. Billy wasn't totally drunk, yet,
but he had a pretty good buzz going. Zeb, on the
other hand, had been out cutting weeds on the back
part of his property behind the family house where he
had lived for over fifty years. Zeb was hot, tired, and
thirsty.

"Bottle of cold Bud," Zeb told Jim Mooney, the
bartender, as he slid onto a barstool about half way
down the bar.

"Comin' up," Mooney said. "What you been doin',
Zeb? Look like you been working too hard."

"Cuttin' weeds."

"Huh? Bad as we need rain, didn't figure even the
weeds would be growing." He set the bottle down in
front of Zeb.

"Damned weeds never quit. I think we could do
without rain for a year, and we'd still have weeds."
He took a long drink. The beer seemed to start
cooling him immediately. "Ah!" he said. "Good
stuff!" He wiped his mouth with the back of his hand.

Billy Jo, who was sitting at the end of the bar, turned around on his barstool so he was parallel to the bar. Billy was known to be the bully in the town of Backswitch. He sat staring at Zeb for a few minutes. "You Zeb Sellers, ain't ya?" he almost growled out.

Zeb slowly turned his head towards Billy. "Yep, sure am."

"Wouldn't be too damned proud of it if I were you. I think you're a crook."

Zeb faced forward again and took another drink. He pushed his old beat-up baseball cap back on his head. "Guess everyone's entitled to their own opinion."

"Ain't no opinion! Everyone knows how you screwed over my granddaddy."

"Never screwed over nobody," Zeb said.

"Well, I say you have, and I think I'm gonna whip your ass."

"No fightin' in here," Jim Mooney said.

Zeb now spun on his stool so he was facing Billy. "Well, sorry you feel that way. I'd really think about that decision, though, if I were you."

"Ain't nothin' to think about. You deserve an ass whippin'!"

"Tell you what, Billy. If you want to save what little pride you have left in this town, I'm gonna give you a chance to change your mind."

182

Billy folded his arms across his chest and leaned back. "And just why would I change my mind?"

"Cause you can't win in a fight with me."

Billy let out a laugh.

"How old are you now?" Zeb asked.

Billy eyed him suspiciously. "Twenty-six." He then paused. "Just what makes you think I can't whip your ass?"

"I didn't say you couldn't whip my ass. I said you couldn't win. I'm seventy-two. You beat me up, I'm gonna tell everyone in the county about you beatin' up an old man. If I beat the tar out'a you, I'll tell everyone in the county you were whipped by an old man. Either way, you lose." Zeb shrugged and took a long pull on his bottle.

Billy took a long drink, too, looked down at the floor, and scratched his head. "Well, looks like I better just buy you another beer and forget fightin'!"

In the Cards

by Sunny Frazier

The Tuesday night poker game was canceled because of Clyde's murder.

I was on patrol when the call came over the box. He was found at his business, an auto repair shop, shot in the head at close range. His wife knew he often stayed late to tinker on cars, so she hadn't checked until after 9 p.m.

In the morning, I broke the news to the other card players, Vince, Leo and Jerry. Two had already heard about the murder on the evening news; Leo reacted with disbelief.

The investigators were satisfied with their suspects: a cheating wife, a teenage son with angst, a neighbor angry because Clyde had reported him for wife abuse. I'd handled that call.

There was no reason for me to add my poker buddies to the suspect list. Jerry and Vince were from the old neighborhood, and nervous enough to be playing cards with a cop. Still, I found myself checking their alibis.

Leo was outside the fire station when I pulled up. "Thanks for calling me with the news. I was sleeping off a two-alarmer we got last night. Abandoned warehouse on the south side burned down."

Vince's alibi was weak. "I was alone all night playing—what else?--video poker. Someday I'm going to bust Leo's lucky streak."

Jerry was nervous when I talked to him. "I told you, I saw it on the news."

"I thought you said your TV was in the shop?"

"I got an old one out in the garage. What's with the interrogation? Who made you a homicide detective?"

Jerry was right. I drank beer with these guys and swapped lies every Tuesday night for three years. I knew them well enough to spot their poker tells. Clyde always sniffed like he had a cold. Vince flicked his tongue across his upper lip. Jerry clamped his jaw so tight the muscle stood out. My poker face was flawless. I should have won more money.

After Clyde was lowered into the grave, we paid condolences to the family and headed for Reilly's Bar. Jerry took a draft and went to a dark corner to drink alone.

"He's taking it hard," Vince commented.

"You'd take it hard, too, if Clyde owed you $500." Leo tossed back a shot of tequila. "You'll never catch me letting somebody walk away owing me money."

Two of Leo's crew joined us. "Great chili you cooked up the other night," one said.

"We needed your help at the fire," said the other. "Where did you go to get the ingredients--Mexico?"

Leo grinned. "I make the best chili in the state. There's a Mexican market across town that sells the freshest habañero peppers, and they're the only ones I'll use. The rest of the ingredients are my secret."

Clyde's home was near the market. I nursed a beer while buying round after round for the others. When Leo headed to the toilet, I followed.

"I thought Clyde owed you money too," I said. "He couldn't come up with the fifty bucks you won with that full house in last week's game."

Leo tried to push past me. "Never happened."

I put my hand on Leo's chest and stared into his eyes. "Are you sure? Because you just said you'd never let anybody walk away owing you money."

That's when I saw it.

Three quick blinks.

Almost a tic. Definitely a tell.

nsportsmanlike Conduct

by BJ Bourg

"I threw for nearly three thousand yards and thirty touchdowns in '79," Andy said to the locals at Rex's Restaurant and Bar. "That record will never be broken."

Jasper pointed to the newspaper clipping on the wall. "Not if he has his way."

Andy glanced at the headline. It read, *Kevin Turner set to break Cut Off High School all-time Quarterback records.* "Kevin got a little lucky once or twice—that's all."

"Lucky?" Jasper's mouth dropped open. "Kevin's thrown twenty-eight touchdowns and over twenty-six hundred yards so far, and he still has two games left to play."

"He won't break any of my records."

"Yes, he will—and I can't wait."

"Look, I'm the best quarterback who ever threw for Cut Off. *Period!*"

"Like I've said a thousand times before; if you were such a great quarterback, why'd you stop at high school ball?"

"Because people are ignorant. They don't know greatness when they see it."

"No," Rex called from behind the bar, "you weren't a team player and everyone knew it."

Andy slammed his bottle of Miller Lite on the bar. "What have any of you ever done that was great? How many of you have your name plastered on the gym wall?"

Jasper turned and nodded to a table of regulars. "We only have to hear this garbage for two more weeks."

Andy kicked back his stool and stormed out the door. His knuckles were white as he drove home, and his heart filled with anger when he drove by the local McDonald's and saw Kevin's red Chevy Z-71 sitting in the shadows of the parking lot. His only claim to fame was about to be washed away by this snot-nosed kid who didn't know the value of a hard day's work. As he stared at the hulking truck, an idea suddenly occurred to him. *If Kevin gets into a little accident, maybe breaks a leg or arm, my record would be safe!* He surveyed the vacant parking lot. He'd have time to pay a quick visit to the truck, cut the brake lines, and drive off before anyone noticed a thing.

***

Thirty minutes later, Andy was settled into his lounge chair. He watched *Law and Order,* but didn't see it. His heart thumped in his chest. He'd never done anything criminal, other than steal fishing lures as a child, and he began to question his actions. His wife hadn't made it home from work and that worried him, too. The proverbial angel floated to his shoulder and taunted him. *What if Kevin killed an innocent person in that monster truck? What if someone saw you cut the brake lines? You'd go to jail for murder! And where is Beth? She's never—*

A knock at the front door startled Andy. He bolted from his chair and his heart fell to his shoes when he saw two cops standing on his front steps. He recognized Sergeant Tim Goldsmith. The other was some new kid. Looked fifteen.

Sergeant Goldsmith cleared his throat. "Andy, I have some bad news."

"What is it?"

"There's been an accident."

Andy's knees grew weak. "Is it Beth?"

Goldsmith nodded. "Kevin lost control of his truck and hit Beth head-on. There was a fire. They were both..."

"Both *what*?"

Goldsmith swallowed hard. "They were both killed."

Andy collapsed to the floor. He gripped his stomach, gasping. A hand touched his shoulder. He looked up. The young cop was staring down at him. "Mr. Turner," the cop said in a choked voice, "I'm so sorry for your loss."

Demon of Pride Tempting a Young Woman

Author Biographies

BJ Bourg is the chief investigator for a Louisiana district attorney's office. He has over fifteen years of law enforcement experience in a variety of fields. BJ has had many stories accepted for publication in over fifteen different venues, including <u>Writer's Post Journal</u>, <u>Mysterical-E</u>, <u>FMAM</u>, <u>Crime and Suspense</u>, and <u>Apollo's Lyre</u>. ePress-Online has published a book of his short stories entitled <u>Absent the Soul</u> and his work has also appeared in the anthology <u>Stories of Strength</u>. In addition to his job and writing, BJ enjoys boxing, martial arts, and shooting. The 35-year-old Louisiana native has received many awards and commendations in his career, but his greatest achievements to date have been the marriage to his wonderful wife and the birth of his two children.

Kimberly Brown's stories have been published in <u>Dreams of Decadence Vampire Fiction and Poetry</u>, <u>Futures Mysterious Anthology Magazine</u>, online at mysterynet.com and flashquake.org, and in a Barnes and Noble anthology, <u>Crafty Cat Crimes</u>. She recently won the <u>Crime and Suspense</u> Random Acts of Crime Contest with her story, "Peace and Quiet." Kimberly and her husband Ed live in the beautiful mountains of Northeast Georgia where their cat, Buffy, rules the roost. When not writing fiction, Kimberly writes for *The Northeast Georgian*, a local newspaper. Kimberly and Ed love to hike, Geocache, and judge for Odyssey of the Mind.

Deborah Elliott-Upton's published credits include Writer's Digest, Woman's World, Great Britain's Fiction Feast, Millennium Science Fiction and Fantasy, Beginnings, Mystery Reader's Journal, newspapers and business trade magazines. A past book reviewer for the Amarillo-Globe News, the internationally-published author is a Personality Trainer, teaches "Writing & Marketing the Short Story" online and at the college level. Five of her short stories were optioned by StarBlaze Entertainment for opening episodes of a proposed television series. When she's not covered in blood writing mysteries, she works as a state-licensed professional killer – an exterminator.

John M. Floyd is the author of more than 500 short stories and fillers in publications like The Strand Magazine, Grit, Pleiades, Woman's World, and Alfred Hitchcock's Mystery Magazine. He was a contributor to the anthology Short Attention Span Mysteries, and an assortment of his short stories are found on Amazon, as Amazon Shorts. A former Air Force captain and IBM systems engineer, he now teaches a number of writing courses online and at a local college. John and his wife Carolyn live in Brandon, Mississippi.

Sunny Frazier has been publishing both fiction and nonfiction since 1972. Her fiction has appeared in Murderous Intent Mystery Magazine, Blue Murder Magazine, Writer's Journal, San Luis Obispo Nightwriters newsletter, and The Line-Up (Fresno County Sheriff's Department magazine). She has also contributed 12 stories to the anthology <u>Valley Fever:</u> <u>Where Murder Is Contagious</u>. She has been writing reviews for the San Joaquin Sisters in Crime newsletter, The Poison Pen, for eight years.

Gary R. Hoffman taught English and Speech/Drama for 22 years in Missouri and California. He quit teaching over 20 years ago to go into business for himself. He now lives in a motor home and says, "Home is where you park it!" He now travels the North American continent, with Sandy and their cat, Callie, and attempts to stay in moderate climates. Gary has recently published a new novel, <u>Death Is</u> <u>Not An Option</u>. He has had short stories published in anthologies, ezines, and magazines, and has won numerous awards for his short stories.

Frank Zafiro's short stories have appeared in small press magazines such as <u>Starsong</u>, <u>Unknowns</u>, <u>GenderiZine of Massachusetts</u> and <u>Wide Open</u> <u>Magazine</u>, as well as online at <u>Ascent Magazine</u>, <u>A</u> <u>Cruel World</u>, <u>Crime and Suspense</u>, <u>SNReview</u>, <u>SaucyVox(dot)Com</u>, <u>Dispatch Literary Journal</u> and <u>Crime Scene Scotland</u>. He is a graduate from Eastern Washington University with a degree in history and works as a police officer in the Pacific Northwest.

The Editor, **Tony Burton**, has been a non-fiction and fiction author for several years. He has two published novels, <u>Blinded By Darkness</u> and <u>A</u> <u>Wicked Good Play</u>, with two more novels in the works. He has published poetry in two anthologies, as well as over 120 newspaper columns and op ed pieces. His short stories have been published online, including in <u>Crime and Suspense</u> and <u>Reflection's Edge</u>. He is the owner/operator/chief cook and bottle washer of Wolfmont Publishing, a small press. Tony has a bachelor's degree in Literature from Excelsior University, a bachelor's degree in Education from Southern Illinois University and a master's degree in Education from Nova University. He lives with his lovely wife, Lara, in rural northwest Georgia.

Author Websites

BJ Bourg
http://www.bjbourg.com

Kimberly Brown
http://www.kimberlybrown.net

Deborah Elliott-Upton
http://www.expressedimagination.com

Sunny Frazier
http://www.sunnyfrazier.com

Gary R. Hoffman
http://www.lulu.com/grhotra

Frank Zafiro
http://www.frankzafiro.com

Tony Burton
http://www.wolfmont.com
http://www.crimeandsuspense.com

Printed in the United States
75193LV00001B/202-237